Eden's Charm

Eden's Charm

A WOMEN OF STAMPEDE NOVEL

C.G. FURST

Happy reading & Best Wishes

C. G. Furst

Published 2018 by C.G.Furst

ISBN: 978-1-7752269-0-1 (Print edition)

Design and Cover Art by Su Kopil, Earthly Charms
Copyediting by Ted Williams

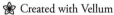 Created with Vellum

DEDICATION

To my family.
Thank you for filling my life with laughter and love.

FOREWORD

I had the privilege of mentoring C.G. Furst through the production of her amazing debut novel *Eden's Charm*. From a tiny seed of an idea, her novel sprouted and blossomed into a dazzling work of fiction. It was a pleasure to watch both C.G. and her novel grow.

C.G. Furst has created a moving and emotional clash between the past, the present and visions of the future. Don't miss your chance to watch a clothing designer mend old hurts and fashion a new life with the cowboy of her dreams.

Katie O'Connor, author of the contemporary romance series, *Hearts Haven: Running Home, Saving Grace and Building Trust.*

ACKNOWLEDGMENTS

I would like to extend a huge thank you to the entire Goodine family for guiding me through the exciting, complex world of rodeo. First, I would like to thank Cole Goodine, who answered endless questions about life as a Bareback rider and was a true inspiration for my rodeo scenes. Cole is a four-time Canadian Finals Rodeo Qualifier, and a 2017 and 2018 Calgary Stampede Qualifier. To Judy Goodine, who graciously agreed to feature her beautiful hand-painted feather on the cover, and to Doug and Kayley Goodine for the behind the scenes details. Thank you, from the bottom of my heart.

Personal thanks to my invaluable readers, Judy, Wendy, Zoe, Hayley and Judy B. for your honesty and constructive input. To my Beta readers, Katie, Shelley and Brenda for their advice, guidance and patience. I couldn't have achieved this without you.

Thanks to Su Kopil of Earthly Charms for designing my beautiful cover and bringing Eden and RJ to life. Thank you also, to Ted Williams for his editing expertise, and to Tammy Jensen of Southern Exposure Photo Studio.

As always, to my husband and family, thank you for your unwavering support throughout this entire process.

And finally, thank you to the Women of Stampede; Katie O'Connor, Shelley Kassian, Brenda Sinclair, Alyssa Linn Palmer, Maeve Buchanan, and Nicole Roy for inviting me along for the ride of a lifetime and making my dreams come true!

CHAPTER 1

*T*here's a slim line between excitement and fear and when it came to RJ Stoke, Eden Blue couldn't seem to find the line. Not today, not tomorrow, or the five long years that had come and gone.

"Breathe, you idiot." Eden thrust a hand through her hair, closed her eyes and inhaled loudly. "Breathe." But the fear continued to clog her throat and immobilize the movement of her limbs. Eden collapsed against the hard edge of a wooden stool over by her workstation at the shopping mall kiosk. Why couldn't she let the panic go? She'd been watching RJ compete in the bareback event since the day he started. She'd seen him thrown to the ground, slammed in the chutes, stomped and kicked and rolled, and he always, always got up with a tip of his hat and a smile for the crowd. Eden buried her head in her hands. She'd watched this particular clip playing on her iPad three times today. It was RJ's winning performance from last week's rodeo in Williams Lake, B.C., and it ended the same way every time. Why couldn't she share the excitement?

"Eighty-six and a half points!" The rodeo announcer's voice boomed from the speaker of the iPad. "That's enough for a move into first place! Please give a big round of applause for this fine young cowboy originating from the Porcupine Hills area of Nanton, Alberta, Ladies and Gentlemen, RJ Stoke—"

"One of the finest cuts of Alberta beef you will ever find."

"RJ?" Eden slowly lifted her head from her hands and came face to face with his warm brown eyes and welcoming smile.

"It's good to see you, Ed."

Eden leapt from the stool and smothered him in a strangling hug. "God, I've missed you, but please, RJ, don't ever call me Ed."

"How about Edie?" he said, looking down at her with an amused lift of an eyebrow.

"How about just Eden?"

"Nope, I like Edie, Eden scares me." His eyes widened in mock fright and Eden punched him in the arm.

"You should be scared, you lily-livered coward, you left me high and dry five years ago and never even called."

"Them's fighting words, Blue. Nobody calls me a lily-livered coward and gets away with it." He squeezed her tight against him and rested his cheek on the top of her head. "Nobody but you, that is. Well, maybe John Wayne or Clint Eastwood could, but that's it." His grin brought back memories of the hours he and Eden had spent devouring movie lines from the old Westerns they'd discovered in the basement at his aunt and uncle's ranch. "Oh, and as I recall, I'm not the only one with a phone. You could have called me."

"I wasn't sure you'd answer." She ducked out from under his chin and met his gaze. "We kind of left things in a mess."

RJ crossed his arms across his chest and shook his head. "Not my finest moment."

"Or mine. Hey, what are you doing here anyway?" she said, trying to draw the conversation away from the pain of the past.

"I'm competing at Stampede." His voice sounded perplexed.

Eden rolled her eyes. "Well, I know that, but Stampede is four days away and you're in Pool B; I wasn't expecting to see you until then."

"I came home early to spend time with Auntie Rae and Uncle Harold and help out at the ranch for a few days. I'm really looking forward to it; I've been away far too long."

"How are they doing?"

"Auntie Rae fell last winter and broke her shoulder. I'm surprised you didn't hear about it. She's fine now, but it was a hard time for both of them." He hitched his thumbs into the front pockets of his jeans and shifted uncomfortably. "I should have been here to help out but I didn't know about it until she was all healed up."

Eden shrugged, straightening a display of Western shirts. "Sounds like they figured it out fine without you. I'm sure the neighbors stepped in and helped out."

"That's not the point." He tipped up the front of his cowboy hat and dark curls spilled across his forehead. "They helped me when I needed them. I should have been here."

"Well, you're here now, I'm sure they'll be over the moon." She tossed him a tight smile, pulled t-shirts from a box beneath the booth's skirting and began folding. She sympathized with his guilt but still wished he was anywhere but here.

"Are you stalking me, Edie?" He pointed to the iPad; his voice flickered with amusement. I overheard my name when I walked over to your booth here."

"No!" Her hand flew to her face covering the rush of heat searing her cheeks. "I was just curious," she hedged, "you know, to see how you've been doing in the standings."

Why, oh why was the mall so quiet right now? Why couldn't there be throngs of people questioning her about the products she was selling so he would promise to get together with her later in the week and just go away. She didn't want to reminisce, not now, not in the middle of the afternoon in a mall in Calgary's downtown core.

RJ winked at her. "You sure that's all it is?" He stepped forward to examine a rack of clothing. Eden tilted her head in an attempt to observe him without being obvious. He was still so handsome it took her breath away. How could a body that was stretched to its limit week after week on the back of a bucking horse remain so straight and strong? When she'd crushed herself against him a few minutes ago, there'd been no mistaking the rigid outline of a very impressive six-pack and rock-hard pecs. Not that she needed to touch him to notice. His tight white t-shirt barely concealed the physical power lying beneath it.

Geez, he might as well be naked. *Shame on you, Eden*, she admonished herself silently. She knew RJ worked out daily to keep his body in top condition for competition. It wasn't vanity that kept him in such good shape, it was part of his job. But damn, it was hard to ignore the total package. Tight, faded Wranglers stretched worn across the most obvious stress points and the slant of his hat with a scattering of loose brown curls peeking below the brim, even the small crescent-shaped scar cradling the corner of his left eye was sexy. No matter how she looked at it, RJ was hot. So very, very hot.

"Did you make these clothes, Edie?" RJ asked pointing at the rack of clothing.

"Yeah, I did." She straightened with pride.

"They're beautiful." He glanced up at a sign burned into a slab of barn wood. "Eden Blue's Country Girl Cow-Tour."

"Couture," she corrected. "It rhymes with manure, something you should be very familiar with."

RJ chuckled heartily. "That I am, I'm usually covered in it." He held up a hanger draped with a faux leather deep mahogany jacket, swinging with fringes and edged with thick silver stitching. "Seriously, Edie, this is gorgeous, you should be selling your clothes on the grounds."

"Thank you." Strange warmth skipped around her heart at the unmistakable pride in his voice. "Maybe in a few years." She smiled and moved closer. "But for now, I'm digging downtown Calgary and Stampede fever." She motioned to the large kiosk enclosed within rustic corral planking and decorated with Western flair. Two large wagon wheels ushered patrons beneath a faux wooden-pole entrance and into a cowboy's shopping paradise. A wall of wooden crates shelved stacks of merchandise, racks of clothing lined the perimeter, and hay bales draped with a flavor of southwestern fabric flanked outhouse-themed change rooms. "We set up a few weeks early and spread the spirit of the West with a line of clothing and souvenirs. By parade day, everyone's pumped for pancakes and parties."

"Who's we?"

"Remember my cousin Kaitlin?"

RJ nodded. "Crazy Kaitlin. She was wilder than any bucking horse I ever rode. I pulled the two of you out of more scrapes than I can remember." He grinned. "I always did like that girl."

"You have to admit, our teenage years were fun," Eden said.

"Maybe for you and Kaitlin but I'm the one who was blamed for your bad behavior."

"Yes, but it cemented your reputation as the troublemaker from Seattle." Eden smiled and wagged a finger at him. "Admit it. You loved it."

"We really had fun." He smiled. "So tell me about Kaitlin. Has she calmed down any?"

"Enough to get married, have two little girls and operate a Western store in High River. I lease a corner for my boutique and work for her full time."

"When do you work on your clothing line?"

"Nights and weekends. I'm a one woman show, RJ."

"One woman, eh?" He stroked his chin. "Does that mean you're still single?"

"Hah, you wish! Get over yourself, buddy, I've had a very satisfying love life since you disappeared." She winced inwardly. Satisfying? Now that was an overstatement. Tepid, lukewarm, bland... five years of lovelorn yuck pretty much summed things up.

His eyes gleamed mischievously. "So you *are* single."

"No, I'm saying it's none of your business." Eden walked to the opposite side of a table in the middle of the kiosk piled with cowboy hats and Western shirts. "But since you asked," she said loudly, "I do have a boyfriend." She turned and collided against him. "Are *you* stalking *me*, RJ?"

"Nope, just curious, I guess."

She pushed against him but he refused to move and grasped her waist when she tried to dodge around him.

"I'd like to meet him while I'm here. What did you say his name was again?" he asked, pulling her towards him.

"I didn't." Eden's lips parted as he brushed away her heavy fringe of cinnamon and golden-hued bangs skirting the crease of her eyelid. She couldn't look away. His lips were so near she could almost taste him. Eden leaned closer. She really, really wanted to taste him.

"Well, well, well, what's going on here?"

An angry female voice and the rustle of shopping bags accompanied by an overpowering aroma of strong floral fragrance sliced through the sensual tug-of-war raging between them.

RJ dropped his hands and adjusted the brim of his hat to shadow the heat in his eyes. "Hey, babe." He leaned over and planted a kiss on the stranger's cheek. "Eden," he said, straightening up and placing his arm around the young woman's shoulders, "this is Velvet Blair—my girlfriend."

Eden bumped against the table sending a stack of cowboy hats toppling to the floor. "Oh sorry, clumsy of me," she sputtered, squatting to retrieve them at the same time RJ bent down to lend a hand. She reached for a Stetson lying at Velvet's feet. Holy crap, her boots were easily twelve hundred dollars. Add the designer jeans, beaded tank and leather jacket and she was well over two grand. Either she was loaded, or RJ had come into a whole lot of money.

Velvet? What kind of name was Velvet? She grabbed the last hat from the floor and placed it on the table. Seriously? And girlfriend? He'd just spent the last ten minutes flirting with her. What was that all about? She breathed in sharply, trying to regain her composure before turning and extending her hand. "It's lovely to meet you."

Velvet arched a perfectly shaped eyebrow at RJ before squaring her hard, cobalt, lined eyes in Eden's direction and coldly touching her outstretched palm. "Likewise," she drawled in a thick, emotionless Texan accent.

"Eden and I were friends in high school. She designs clothing—"

"Yes," Eden interrupted, "and R J has chosen some beautiful items for you." She strode to her rack of clothing and selected several of her pricier items; an edgy vest in tobacco leather with looped stitching and a black fringed V neckline, a soft wool shawl jacket in a southwest inspired blue, rust and cream design, and a very expensive pair of very short 'Daisy Dukes', strategically torn and frayed. "This vest will accentuate your eyes." Hard cruel eyes, she noted, black as coal with a tinge of purple. Shit. Even her eyes were beautiful.

"Thank you, RJ, you're so sweet. These are all lovely, but I'd adore this piece, too." Her fingers lingered on a simple, but incredibly soft royal blue long-sleeved cardigan with a swingy fringed hem.

"Oh, I'm sorry. This is a gift for RJ's aunt. He picked it out earlier. Isn't that right, RJ?"

"Sure did." His voice was terse and a flicker in his eyes warned her to back off. Eden wrinkled her nose. Two could play this game, and she'd be damned to be the one to back off first.

"RJ, look at this." Velvet wrapped a hand-tooled leather belt around her hips. "It's too big for me, of course." She laughed. "But it's really nice and I think you should get it for your uncle. Try it on. I want to see if it looks as good on you as it does on me." She circled it around his body, threading it over the large silver buckle and belt looped through his jeans, purposely stroking her fingers across his butt. "It's perfect." She stepped back for a better look. "You're perfect." She reached forward and draped her arms protectively around his neck calling over his shoulder to Eden. "We'll take this too, hon."

"Great. I'll wrap it up." Eden yanked the belt from between their squashed hips and stalked over to the cash register. She tossed the belt in a bag and began ringing in his purchases.

Okay, she got it. Velvet was staking her claim, letting her know RJ was off limits. "Thanks so much for your business." She ripped the receipt from the debit machine and shoved it in his hand. "Oh, and I gave you ten percent off." Her eyes flashed angrily. "Stampede special."

"Well, thank you." He tipped his hat. "It was lovely seeing you again, dear. I'll give you a call and we can set up a supper date. I can't wait to meet your boyfriend."

Eden shoved her copper chin length bob behind her ears and grimaced as RJ and Velvet sauntered hand in hand down the mall. "You and me both, RJ, I can't wait to meet him too."

CHAPTER 2

"*A*re you sure her name isn't Vulva?"

"Stop it, that's disgusting!" Eden clapped a hand across her mouth and collapsed against the well-worn sofa cushions, convulsing with laughter. "Okay, enough." She swiped the tears from her cheeks, peeked at Kaitlin and burst out laughing all over again. "We have to stop," she gasped, the palm of her hand covering the rim of her wine glass, protection from the imminent crimson splatter. "We'll wake the girls."

"Oh, they'll sleep through anything; it's getting them to go to bed that's the problem. I didn't dare tell them you were coming over tonight."

"I'm sorry I missed seeing them. I love those little muffins." She truly enjoyed spending time with Kaitlin and Luke Frazer's little girls. Molly and Josie were five and three years old and had boundless energy; a trait inherited from their mother's wild side, a trait Eden was quick to point out to Kaitlin. Eden loved them to bits, especially at dusk, when they'd clamor up onto the sofa, warm and fragrant from their evening bath, snuggle against her in their cozy pjs, each clutching a blankie to cuddle and book for Eden to read.

"They're not muffins! They're monsters! Golden-haired, blue-eyed monsters with sticky fingers and dirty shoes—"

"—and funny questions, and big grubby hugs. They're adorable," Eden gushed.

Kaitlin slid deeper into the cushions, closed her sky blue eyes and shook her head side to side. "They have you so brainwashed. I'm going to grab Luke and take off for a week. A whole week, and leave you here all by your lonesome." She pointed an index finger in Eden's direction. "Then you'll see how adorable they are." She placed her empty water bottle on the coffee table, shifted to a sitting position and leaned back against the arm of the sofa, drawing her knees up to her chest and circling them with her arms. "Enough about my angelic children, let's get back to Vulva."

"Her name is Velvet and as much as I hate to admit it, I kind of like the name. It's pretty."

"Pretty awful if you ask me." She twisted her mouth in thought. "So, is she red velvet or black velvet?"

"What are you talking about?"

"Red velvet is like something smooth and delicious like a plate of red velvet cupcakes. Mouth-watering and delectable, every crumb a morsel of perfection, twelve silky confections to savor and soothe, and before you know it you've devoured the whole dozen and licked the plate clean." Kaitlin rubbed her belly and smacked her lips. "On the other hand, black velvet evokes darkness and sin. It's smooth like red velvet, but slinky, you know, like a panther concealed in the shadows waiting to pounce."

Eden sat in stunned silence. "Wow, you're really overthinking this."

"I'm trying to get Vulvanized."

"You're trying to get me in trouble! Every time I see her now I'll think of that horrible name. What if I call her Vulva instead of Velvet?"

"Please let me be there when you do!" Kaitlin laid her head on her knees and burst into laughter. "Okay," she finally gulped, raising her head from her knees and wiping tears from her face, "I could use a cup of tea." She rose and tripped over a pair of tiny cowboy boots abandoned in her path. "See how precious your little muffins are now?"

Eden smiled. Kaitlin and Luke's home had always been, in Kaitlin's own words, 'chosen chaos'. Tucked beneath a grassy knoll, and sheltered by lush towering hedges on an acreage west of High River, the property's remarkable beauty outshone its worn and crumbling present. It was a serene, sometimes chaotic lifestyle and it was everything Eden still dreamed her life would have been if RJ hadn't ended their relationship and left for Texas, five years ago.

Eden watched Kaitlin reach for a teapot on the counter and fill her mug. Kaitlin sipped the hot beverage and smiled. "Mmm, hits the spot. More wine? She grabbed a bottle of red from the counter and pushed the cowboy boots aside on her way back to the sofa. "Luke's a great dad but his housekeeping skills could use a kick in the ass." She refilled Eden's wine glass and sat back down. "Tell me more about rodeo's sexiest man alive. What's RJ like now?"

"He's not scrawny anymore." Eden paused, reflecting on the image of his tight white tee and Wranglers, "He's filled out spectacularly."

"Well, he may look good on the outside but from what you told me on the phone earlier he sounds like a jerk."

"We caught each other off guard." Eden sighed. "It was great to see him and he seemed happy to see me, too and this may sound stupid, but when he held me in his arms, it felt like old times, like we'd never been apart."

Kaitlin gripped her arm. "Don't. He hurt you. Don't you remember the pain you went through when he cheated on you? You were a wreck, and I won't ever let him hurt you again."

"I just said it felt like we'd never been apart." She paused. "And I think he felt that way too. Otherwise why would he flirt with me when he knew I'd find out about Vul—vet. It doesn't make any sense." Eden raised her glass to her lips for a sip of wine before laying her head against the soft, faux leather sofa cushions. "We both acted like children. It's embarrassing. But you know what hurts the most? Just before he left, he said to me, 'It was lovely seeing you again, dear.'" She turned in her cousin's direction. "Who says that?"

"What guy says something like that? Great-aunt Melinda says it sometimes."

"Exactly. But, I'm not a seventy-year-old lady. Why would you say that to someone you once loved?" Eden wiped a tear from her cheek. "It was condescending."

Kaitlin scooted across the cushions and gathered Eden in her arms. "I'm sorry, hon, maybe it's a Texas expression, like a term of endearment."

Eden leaned her head against her cousin's shoulder and smiled weakly through her tears. "Maybe, but it made me feel like we'd never been a couple, like I was an insignificant part of his past." More tears rolled down her cheeks. "I'm sorry." She pulled away and used her shirt sleeve to mop the moisture from her face.

"You have nothing to be sorry about. Come on." She pulled Eden from the sofa and dragged her down the hallway towards the bathroom. "Look," she said, both hands planted on the side of Eden's head, directing her towards the mirror.

"At what?"

"At you. You're beautiful. You shouldn't let anyone make you feel anything less, especially someone like RJ."

"You haven't seen Velvet." She shot a baleful reflective glance at her cousin.

"So, what does the Vulvinator have that you don't?"

"Hair. Gobs of thick, glossy black hair down to here." Eden slid her hands along her torso, clipping in at her waist. "Oh, and she has eyes you can drown in, tinged in purple, at least that's what it looked like and she's thin and tall and has breasts the size of melons."

"And?"

"And I don't."

Kaitlin cupped her face. "When I look into your eyes, I feel like I'm falling through a summer sky and your hair is—"

"Yeah, I know. My hair is falling in cheeky little waves that dance along my chin," she groaned, mocking the stylist who had cut her hair. "I'm never going to that salon again. Look what he did to me, I look like I'm fourteen!"

"You look like a successful fashion designer. Who else could get away with shades of cinnamon and gold and make it look like you were born that way?"

"You could."

"Well yeah, but I'm your cousin. We share the same genes."

Eden shrugged at her image in the mirror, then turned away and tugged on her cousin's blonde braid. "Thanks, I guess. But I still feel like crap." They walked arm in arm back to the kitchen and, after retrieving their drinks, pulled a couple of stools up to the island.

"I told RJ I had a boyfriend," Eden confided, silently tracing the intricate swirls embedded in the quartz countertop with her fingertips.

"What?"

"He was teasing me about being single and I lied to him." She dropped her head into her hands. "What am I going to do? RJ wants to meet my fake boyfriend." A door slammed in the distance and her head snapped to attention.

"Anybody home?" A deep voice rumbled across the house.

"We're in the kitchen, honey," Kaitlin yelled.

"What's going on in here?" Luke strolled around the corner, rolling up the sleeves of his shirt as he walked towards them. He bent and kissed Kaitlin on the lips. "Hi, beautiful."

"Hi, yourself." Their eyes met and held. "I didn't expect you until later tonight."

"The flight from Fort Mac got in early." He flipped open the door of the refrigerator, pulled out containers of leftovers and popped them into the microwave to heat, then opened a beer. He nodded towards Eden. "What's wrong with you? You look like shit."

She grimaced. "Back at ya, Luke."

"Eden's ex is in town and he wants to meet her boyfriend."

"You have a boyfriend? When did that happen?" The microwave dinged and he helped himself to a large helping of food from the containers. "Mmm, this is so good, honey," he said between bites, "camp food doesn't compare." He shoveled in a couple more mouthfuls and waved his fork at Eden. "Who's the new guy?"

"There isn't one. I made him up."

"Seriously?" He slapped his hand against the countertop and roared with laughter. "Oh man, that's a good one. What are you going to do now?"

"I don't know." Eden plunked her elbow on the counter. "Any ideas?"

"There's got to be someone we know who will play along for a few days." Kaitlin scrunched up her face, deep in thought. "How about Jon?"

"Jon? My brother Jon? I don't think he's Eden's type."

Eden dropped her hand and sat up straight. "He doesn't have to be my type. He only has to pretend to be for one night, that's all. And he and I know each other. It's perfect." She high-fived Kaitlin. "Thanks, cuz."

"Before you start celebrating, you should probably ask Jon," Luke reasoned with a raised eyebrow. "He could be in a relationship for all we know."

"Oh, for heaven's sake, Luke, you'd know if your brother was in a relationship." Kaitlin scolded.

"Last time we talked he was chatting up some girl at work. Just saying."

"I'll talk to him tomorrow." Eden high-fived Kaitlin once more, the fringe of her cheeky little waves bouncing a happy dance along her chin and plans for 'operation RJ' formulating in her brain.

CHAPTER 3

"Sugar, I don't like that girl," Velvet complained.

"What girl would that be?" RJ padded through the doorway of his childhood bedroom, naked from the waist up, a fluffy white towel slung low around his hips. He closed the door and slid both hands through his hair, brushing damp curls from his face.

Velvet yawned and stretched, twisting her dark tousled tresses on top of her head and shaking a tumbling cascade across her creamy shoulders. A thin gauzy fabric clung to her full, firm breasts. "You know darn well what girl, the one at the mall."

"You mean Eden?" he asked over his shoulder as he applied deodorant. "Why not? Everyone likes Eden." He turned to look at Velvet.

Her eyes were icy. "She's in love with you."

A smile tipped his mouth. "Eden and I are ancient history." He sauntered slowly towards her. "You've got nothing to worry about, babe." He reached over and tenderly stroked the side of her face.

"Oh, believe me, I'm far from worried." She tilted her head confidently. "I happen to know what you like." Her hands seductively circled his pecs, his nipples hardening instantly under her

15

practiced palms, "and how you like it. Mmm." A slip of her tongue, warm and wet, torched a rush of shivers across his taut layer of abs. "You're like a sip of sin, RJ," she moaned, pressing her perfectly French-tipped manicure along the soft edge of cotton circling his waist, "you're burning me, baby. C'mon, help me put the fire out." Her lips brushed the length of his erection vividly outlined beneath the towel.

RJ groaned, grasped her hands and pressed them firmly against his throbbing bulge. "Oh, babe," he groaned again. "As much as I like where this could be headed, I'm not entirely comfortable making love to you with my aunt downstairs making breakfast."

"But she's downstairs—" She pouted dramatically.

"And this is a very old house." He smiled and wove his fingers through her silky mane. "Sound travels. Sound I'd rather not share with my aunt and uncle. You know darn well how noisy things get when we get carried away."

"Your loss," she pouted, flopping miserably up against the soft pillows and drawing a cotton sheet over her breasts.

"We'll have plenty of time for ourselves when Stampede starts, Velvet. Once we're at the hotel I'll give you anything you want."

"Anything, RJ?" she asked with a wicked curve of the lips, "because *you know* what I really want."

"And you know how much I love giving it to you."

"I can't wait to have you all to myself." Her eyes flitted around the bedroom, "I wish we had our own bathroom. I hate sharing with strangers."

RJ smiled and sat beside her on the bed. "Make some room for me."

"I knew you'd come to your senses." She inched slowly to the center of the double bed and drew her tousled mane over her shoulder. "Can't say no to your pretty baby, can you?"

"Usually, no." He brushed her lips gently with his. "But I need you to understand our situation."

Muffled laughter from downstairs filtered up through the

furnace vents in the floor. "See what I mean? All I'm asking is for you to indulge me for a few days and when we have our own space, I'll make everything up to you."

Velvet sighed and pressed her head against his shoulder. "You're damn right you will, and this space better come with its very own ensuite or you're in serious trouble, cowboy."

"It will, don't you worry." He chuckled and stroked a hand along the silk of her hair. "I love to please you, Velvet, you know that."

A stream of early morning sun stealthily bathed the bedroom in a golden hue. "Hey, I want to show you something." RJ grasped Velvet by the wrist and pulled her from the comfort of the bed over to the open window. Morning dew glistened on grass-covered hills and towering pines swayed in the gentle breeze beneath the distant majesty of the Rocky Mountains. Cattle grazed in the nearby pastures that surrounded a large red hip-roof barn and adjoining corrals. "Pretty, huh?" He inhaled the crisp morning air deep into his lungs. "Man, it's good to be home."

"It's beautiful. I can certainly understand your desire to visit."

"You know, Velvet, someday it would be a wonderful place to raise a family." He tightened his embrace around her waist and his lips grazed the curve of her ear.

She snuggled close and lifted a hand to stroke the side of his cheek. "I'm sure it would be, hon, but I'm not convinced I could leave my home and family to live in Canada. My future's in Texas and you know it. Daddy expects me and my brother William to take over Blair Oil and Gas in the near future. He also suggested you'd be a wonderful asset to our ranching operations someday."

"Oh, he did, did he? You didn't happen to put a bug in his ear, did you?"

Velvet's lips curled in a smile. "Perhaps, but you should know Daddy trusts you and admires your strong work ethic. I know you're sentimental being home with your aunt and uncle and all, but I like having you around. We're a good team, RJ, and we belong together in Texas, not here on the ranch."

A sudden gust of wind swirled along the driveway and his gaze followed a tiny piece of crimson cloth swirling along the gravel until it snagged in the thick underbrush beneath the pines. It reminded him of Eden's hair.

Velvet flinched and coldly turned to face him, "Is there another reason you've been so anxious to return to your precious little ranch?"

"Such as?"

"A pretty little red head?"

"The only reason I'm home is because I earned the right to compete at the Calgary Stampede. Eden has nothing to do with it. Now," he said, patting her on the bottom and smiling, "I have to go help Uncle Harold with chores." He dropped the towel from around his hips and pulled on his boxer briefs and jeans. "It'd be nice," he said, fastening the buttons on his shirt, "if you helped Auntie Rae make breakfast."

"Sure thing, sugar. I'll be down right after my shower." She blew him a kiss, plucked her robe off the chipped surface of a chair in the corner of the room and crossed through the doorway on her way to the *only* bathroom on the second floor.

CHAPTER 4

Five framed photos lined the wall above the antique black-washed sideboard in his aunt's dining room. A rodeo still of RJ riding the hell out of a bucking horse, RJ and Uncle Harold outlined in silhouette herding cattle along a tree-lined vista at dusk, Auntie Rae and RJ sharing a laugh at a backyard barbecue; and Kaitlin, RJ and Eden, fierce and proud, strutting arm in arm between the rows of chairs lining the high school auditorium at graduation. Four photos garnered a smile and warmed his heart, but it was the fifth photo, the large black and white in the middle that made his heart go still.

"I thought I'd find you here." Auntie Rae soundlessly appeared behind him and slipped an arm around his waist. "I heard you come down a few moments ago. Your uncle never did fix that creaky step third from the bottom." Her eyes twinkled. "It's a dead giveaway every time."

"I used to try and avoid it when I came in past curfew." He caught her eye and they chuckled together.

Her blue-gray gaze returned to the black and white photo centered on the wall. "Can you believe it's been eight years since your parents passed, RJ?"

They somberly reflected on the last day RJ had seen his parents alive. "If I hadn't gone home with Grandpa Stoke from the beach that day I would have been in the accident, too." RJ swallowed and pushed past the lump forming in his throat. "It was the best day and worst night of my life. How do you reconcile something like that?"

"I'm not sure you ever do." She sighed and rested her hand against his arm. "You carry on the best you can, I guess. Isn't that what the experts say? Tuck away the good memories so the bad ones slowly fade? I don't know. I think of your mom every day, thankful for the number of years we shared. You and I were blessed. I shared fifty years with my younger sister, and you…" she swallowed hard. "…you had fifteen wonderful years with both your parents. They were good people, RJ, and you're living, breathing proof of the morals and values they instilled in you as a child. They did a worthy job."

"You forgot to add that my aunt and uncle went beyond the call of duty taking me in when I had no place to go." He embraced her.

"Didn't want to blow my own horn," she goaded good-naturedly.

"Considering the circumstances, you should." RJ smiled at her. "Auntie Rae, you and Uncle Harold turned my life around. I love Grandpa Stoke and he was doing the best he could after the accident, but he was grieving the loss of his only son and I was too selfish to notice. I still cringe when I think of everything I put him through. Coming home drunk and stoned, skipping school. It's no wonder he shipped me off from Seattle. How could I get into trouble here?" He chuckled. "You live in the middle of nowhere."

"We like to think of it as heaven on earth." She laid a hand on his arm. "Don't be too hard on yourself. You were fifteen, grieving, and making terrible choices. We just happened to be your best option."

RJ pulled her into a hug. "If anything ever happens and you

need help, I hope you'll turn to me. I want to be your best option someday, too."

"You're not an option, RJ, you're the best thing that ever happened to us and the first person we'd turn to in times of trouble."

"You didn't turn to me when you broke your shoulder."

"I wouldn't call that trouble, just a minor inconvenience. Besides, it gave me a good excuse to order your uncle around." She laughed and threw him a wink. "He treated me like a queen and he learned how to cook something other than bacon and eggs. It really was a win-win for me."

"Uncle Harold needed help checking cattle and doing chores. You should have called."

"We had plenty of help from the neighbors, don't you worry, son."

Son.

The threat of tears pricked behind his eyes. His aunt and uncle had never treated him as anything less. He'd been furious when his grandfather had ripped him away from the only life he had known by putting him on a plane to Calgary, and sending him from his home in Seattle to live with his relatives, Rae and Harold Benson, in Alberta. Although his mom and aunt had remained close and had talked monthly on the phone, money was tight on both sides and running back and forth across the border to visit was a luxury neither family could afford. At the airport he'd been met by a couple he had scarcely remembered. He'd been beyond pissed and had reacted to their welcome as a sullen, rude and ungrateful brat.

If his aunt and uncle had been concerned about his attitude the first couple of weeks he'd spent at the ranch, it had never shown. Each morning he had begrudgingly helped with chores before disappearing for the rest of the day into his bedroom to plot his escape. RJ shook his head in disgust; every detail of that part of his life had remained permanently etched in his brain, almost like it'd happened yesterday…

"I'm living in country Hell. You gotta help me outa here."

He texted in vain, a daily plea to friends equally as broke and who really didn't care.

When his friends stopped texting him back, he was determined more than ever to launch a plan to leave the ranch. In the two weeks he'd been there, he'd almost managed to "borrow" enough money from his aunt's purse for a bus ticket to Seattle. He was sprawled on his bed carefully counting the money when he heard a vehicle crunch along the gravel driveway and Auntie Rae call up the stairs asking him to go outside and help his uncle unload a parcel. Hurriedly, he scooped his stash into a Ziploc bag and stowed it in a duffel bag in the back of the closet before heading out to the yard.

Loud thumps rocked the stock trailer hooked up to the truck and Uncle Harold was nowhere in sight. RJ cautiously approached, curious to see what was causing the commotion. He gingerly hopped on the running board and peered inside. Two large, rage-filled eyes glared back. The animal pawed the trailer floor, snorted and lunged forward, scaring the shit out of him. He cursed as he hit the ground and was in the process of dusting himself off when his uncle appeared around the side of the truck.

"There you are. I need your help with something." He waved a hand for RJ to follow and disappeared around the back of the trailer stopping at the passenger door on the opposite side. "Hold the door while I untie the halter on this critter, she's a little finicky, doesn't like traveling much."

Inside, the trailer was dark, and the open door didn't cast much light on what kind of 'critter' his uncle was untying. "Okay, now go round back and open both doors and I'll lead her out." RJ did what he was told and stood as far to the side of the stock trailer as possible, ready to scramble into the corral if he had to.

"Just like a woman to make a big fuss about nothing," his uncle muttered, shaking his head as he led a surprisingly quiet, large white horse with dark brown markings onto the gravel.

"What did you say, Harold?" Auntie Rae scowled as she strolled up to inspect the new horse.

He grinned sheepishly at his wife. "She's a beauty, eh?"

"That's not what you said." She wagged a finger at him and pulled back a smile. "But I'll let it go just this once." She gently stroked the animal's neck. "Well, you are a beauty." She turned towards the corral. "Come meet Polly, RJ, She's an American Paint Horse."

RJ warily stepped forward and put out his hand. Polly whinnied; her long dark mane brushed his fingers as she lowered her head and nudged his shoulder with her nose.

Uncle Harold chuckled as RJ jumped back from the horse's prodding. "She's checking you out," he said, "probably hoping you've got a treat."

"What kind of treat?"

"An apple or a carrot—"

"Which I just happen to have." Auntie Rae reached into her pocket, produced a couple of carrots and handed them to RJ. "You're about to become her new best friend."

He held up a carrot and Polly snatched it away with her teeth, chomping greedily while searching for another. A huge smile creased his face as she tickled his outstretched palm with the coarse whiskers lining her smooth wet lips. "Where did you get her?"

"Our neighbor, Fred Handers, was talking about taking her to auction. I've been looking for a ranch horse with a good temperament for awhile now and Polly fit the bill so I snapped her up. Could you help me look after her RJ?"

"Uh…"

"I've been watching you with the other horses during chores and I like the way you respect their space. I'll be busy haying this week and won't have time to make Polly feel welcome. I sure would appreciate it if you would do it for me."

"Uh…" He hesitated, pondering what to do. He still didn't have enough money for a bus ticket. Polly nudged his shoulder and whinnied. It would probably take a couple of weeks or so to get the *money to leave. Looking after a horse wouldn't be so bad, at least he wouldn't have to spend time talking with his aunt and uncle. "I guess. What do I do?"*

"I'll teach you. But first, let's show Polly her new home."

His uncle offered up the halter rope and RJ grasped it tightly, then stepped towards the barn and was tugged to the ground when the horse yanked back and refused to move. With raised brows, he wordlessly questioned his uncle.

"Click your tongue. Like this." Uncle Harold demonstrated clicking his tongue against the roof of his mouth.

RJ scrambled to his feet, clicked his tongue and Polly obligingly plodded ahead.

"That's the way, RJ, you just have to show her who's boss."

"And sometimes you just need to give her a good tap on the rump," Auntie Rae added wryly when RJ was out of earshot.

"Just like you, my dear," Harold quipped with a grin and then quickly dodged beyond her reach.

"Earth to RJ," Auntie Rae said, jabbing him playfully in the ribs.

He smiled down at her. "Sorry, I was thinking about the day Uncle Harold brought Polly home."

"That was the first time you showed any interest in the ranch." She grinned and pointed to his graduation photo. "Do you have any plans to catch up with Eden and Kaitlin while you're here?"

"Yeah, I ran into Eden yesterday at the mall and made plans to meet her for supper."

"I'm happy to hear that, it's important to stay in touch with old friends." She patted his arm, "Now go outside and find your uncle. Breakfast is almost ready and I don't want it to get cold."

∾

"SUGAR, could you give me a lift back to Calgary today?" Velvet's head popped above the top rail of the corral.

RJ frowned and dropped the chop bucket. Clouds of silt drifted over his boots and coated the bottom of his jeans. "What's going on? We just got here last night. I thought the plan was to go back to Calgary on Tuesday."

"Margo Kennedy called. She and Justine Morgan booked a three-day trip to Banff and invited me along."

"We came here to spend time with my aunt and uncle so they could get to know you." He tipped back his hat and rubbed the sweat from his brow with his shirt sleeve. If the morning temperature was any indication, today was going to be a scorcher. He didn't need Velvet turning up the heat and selfishly changing his plans.

"I know, sugar." She pursed her lips in a pretty red pout. "But you're going to be working every day with your uncle, and you know I'm *dying* to see Banff."

RJ gritted his teeth. "And I won't have time to show it to you, will I?"

"That's what I thought, too," she agreed brightly. "I know I should have asked before accepting, hon, but I knew you wouldn't mind. I mean your poor aunt is stuck planning something for her and me to do all day. She's lovely RJ, but I can tell from our conversations she's itching to weed her garden and clean up around the house. Plain and simple, I'm in her way."

"You could offer to help her, you know?" He strode through the corral gate and latched it behind him.

"When have I ever mopped a floor or dug in the dirt?" She jumped to the ground and fluttered her brightly painted fingernails in his face. "Never have, never will." She smiled and brushed her lips against the crescent-shaped scar near his left eye, "I just want to have a little fun, is that too much to ask?"

"Yes, Velvet, it is. My aunt and uncle have been planning our visit for months and they're excited we're staying at the ranch for a few days. I've been working my ass off all year so you can have fun whenever you want. I think it's time you did something nice in return."

"Sugar." She lifted an eyebrow and cupped his face in her hands. "I didn't come all this way to sit on a porch in the middle of nowhere and fan myself in the heat. When I get back from Banff and we have time alone I'll do something *very nice* for you and you'll forget all about this little spat." Her lips curved in a smile. "Besides, it's not like I won't be spending time with your aunt and uncle at the rodeo, and I'm sure they'll be more than happy to have you all to themselves for a few days. You can reminisce about old times, all day and all night if you want and I won't have to worry about being bored. Now, Margo and Justine are waiting for me in Calgary and I need a ride. Are you going to drive me or do I ask your uncle?"

CHAPTER 5

*E*den paused outside the door of Kaitlin's brother-in-law's office and nervously wiped the palms of her hands along the fabric of her skirt. A series of deep breaths caught in her throat and did little to calm the anxious thump in her chest. When she'd woken this morning, the idea to approach Jon and ask him to pose as her boyfriend didn't seem like a great concept anymore. But it was the only plan she had to convince RJ her life was complete without him. She had no choice but to forge ahead. Eden breathed in sharply and poked her head around the door. "Knock, knock."

"One sec." Jon raised a hand in acknowledgment and continued to type on his computer, barely missing a beat.

She entered the office and glanced around the room, her eyes drawn to the broad stream of sunlight pouring through enormous panes of glass and painting the office in bold strokes of white light. To the left, Jon's desk was a massive construction zone. Maps, reference books and a dizzying number of colorful flagged contracts overlapped the torn-out business section of the morning newspaper. She linked her fingers behind her back and scrutinized three professionally framed photos depicting Calcore's northern holdings.

"Sorry for the wait. How can I help you?" He glanced up impatiently.

Eden cringed. Jon was obviously annoyed at her interruption. This was such a bad idea.

"Eden Blue." His face brightened. "What a nice surprise." He rose, closed the distance between them and enveloped her in a hug. "What brings you to the big city?"

"Kaitlin has a kiosk at Bow Valley Square for Stampede. I'm working a shift today."

"Right, Luke mentioned she was doing that again this year. Wow, it's great to see you. Have a seat." He released her and gestured towards a couple of mustard-toned vinyl armchairs in front of his desk. "What's it been, two, three months?" He lifted an index finger. "Wait. Kait and Luke's branding at the end of May, now I remember." His mouth parted in a dazzling smile displaying even white teeth. "What's going on?"

Eden adjusted her posture, gripped the seat cushion, and leaned forward. "I need to borrow something."

Jon waved a hand in the air. "Name it. Whatever you need it's yours."

"You." Eden swallowed and cleared her throat. "I need to borrow you."

"Uhh—me?" Jon sank back in his chair and slid a hand through his short blonde, meticulously groomed hair. "How so?"

"My ex is in town for Stampede. He's competing in the bareback event and he wants to meet my boyfriend."

"I think you better start at the beginning because I'm not following." His brow wrinkled.

"I don't have a boyfriend, Jon," she blurted. "He caught me off guard, teasing me about being single and before I knew it I was confessing I had a boyfriend. Worse still, he's got a girlfriend and she's gorgeous." Eden sighed.

"And you're not?"

"Oh boy, not even close."

Jon smiled and touched her gently on the arm. "Don't sell yourself short, Eden, you're a beautiful woman."

His touch and the sincerity in his voice did little to lift her spirits. "Am I beautiful enough to be your girlfriend?"

"Whoa, that makes me sound shallow." He dropped his hand to his lap and leaned back in his chair.

"This is so wrong. I'm sorry, Jon, I shouldn't have asked." She nervously bunched the fabric of her skirt, smoothed it out again and abruptly stood. "I'll come clean with RJ when he phones. Don't worry, it'll be fine." She hurried towards the door. "Thanks for your time. It really was nice to see you again."

Behind her, Jon sighed heavily. "What are you doing after work tonight?"

"Huh?" She whirled to face him.

His face crinkled at her stunned response. "If I'm going to be your boyfriend, we should probably get to know each other better."

A GUST of warm July wind ushered Eden through the door of Rooney's Irish Pub tossing her hair in tangled disarray. Jon waved from a small corner booth on the opposite side of the room. She paused, smoothed her hair and smiled brightly at the sight of him draining a glass of deep black liquor. Something decidedly Irish she concluded.

A smile tugged at her lips at the memory of their first meeting on Skype five years ago. As an engineer for Calcore Energy, Jon had been overseas, supervising the assembly of an offshore drilling rig and she had been stuck at home trying to organize maid of honor *and* best man duties for Kaitlin and Luke's wedding. Thankfully they'd hit it off immediately. Jon was goofy, lighthearted and totally hot. In fake-boyfriend terms, he was the complete package and guaranteed to fool even the toughest opponents, including RJ.

"Hi." She casually scanned her surroundings. "This is nice. I've never been here before."

A rich combination of solid mahogany woodwork, stunning stained-glass inserts, and Celtic floor mosaics cast a true Irish ambiance under the soothing amber glow of magnificent antique chandeliers. She slid into the booth and placed her purse on the space between them. "Sorry I'm late. I had a customer who couldn't decide between a yellow t-shirt and a blue t-shirt."

Jon smiled. "And?"

"Blue won." She grinned. "Last sale of the day, didn't want her to walk away empty- handed so I may have influenced her decision." She pointed a finger at him. "But in my humble, professional, fashionista opinion, blue was by far the better choice."

"You've got moxie, Red."

Her grin immediately faded and her fingers fumbled through her hair.

"What? Shit. What'd I say wrong?"

"My ex's girlfriend has the most beautiful long black hair and I'm stuck with a stringy red mop."

"Well, in case you haven't noticed, your hair has been red since I've known you."

"Cinnamon, copper, russet, auburn, ginger," she listed, tapping the fingertips of her opposite hand, "not red."

"What's the deal? Everyone has colored hair these days—pink, blue, purple, if you ask me red's pretty normal."

"It's different when you grow up with it."

"You could always change the color. Why do you hate it so much?"

"In a word, Sammy Turner, grade one through seven. He used to call me carrot top and tomato head and any other mean thing he could think of."

"I'm surprised Kaitlin didn't beat him up."

"She did. But he wouldn't stop. I was ecstatic when his family moved."

"He probably had a crush on you."

"Trust me. He enjoyed making my life miserable." Eden wrinkled her nose and sighed. "And you know what? I actually like the color of my hair, but yesterday when RJ showed up with Miss Texas on his arm, all the bad stuff came rushing back."

He shook his head. "You need alcohol. Bad."

"A glass of wine would be perfect."

"White or russet?"

"Smart ass." She tossed him a smile. "Make it a russet."

EDEN ABSENTLY BIT the top of a French fry. The next time she had a bad day she was definitely coming back to Rooney's for the soothing atmosphere. Snuggled in the small booth alongside Jon was like being wrapped in a cozy hug. "This is a great place to meet up with friends."

"Yeah, I guess."

"No, it is. It says right here on the menu." She tapped the vinyl coating with her finger. "'A great place to meet up with friends, warm and inviting, a true Irish experience'."

He raised an eyebrow. "Are you going to eat that piece of fish?" She pushed her plate towards him and he stabbed the batter-coated fillet with his fork. "Best fish and chips in the city," he commented between bites.

Eden smiled. Jon was adorable even if he did have a tiny smidge of tartar sauce smeared along the bottom half of his chin. He snatched her finger when she reached to wipe it away, brought it to his lips and kissed the tip.

"Um, what are you doing?"

"You mean this?" He nibbled the tip with his teeth, refusing to let go as she tried to yank it away.

"I think we need to establish some rules."

"Fake boyfriend rules?"

"Yes. Fake boyfriend rules, because that's what you are. My fake boyfriend."

"Too bad." He leaned forward, his gray-green eyes shining mischievously. "Because, you taste delicious."

"Okay." She laughed and tugged her finger from his grip. "You've passed the fake boyfriend test. You're a great fingertip nibbler."

"That's not all I'm great at." Eden rolled her eyes and Jon's lips tipped in a grin. "Okay, he said. "What are the rules?"

"I'm not really sure." She tilted her head and lifted her shoulders in question. "Hmm, let's see. No kissing."

"We might have to kiss to make our relationship look authentic. You won't be disappointed. I've been told I'm a pretty good kisser."

"Me, too." She wrinkled her nose. "I don't see a kiss happening but if it does we'll have truly great fake kisses."

"What else?"

"No touching body parts."

"Like finger nibbling?"

"If you don't want to do this—"

"I'm sorry, I do." He stifled a laugh. "But I think we should figure things out as they happen, like if we're dancing somewhere there's a pretty good chance we'll bump body parts and—" he paused and cleared his throat, making her wonder what he was thinking. "Uh, I think we need to establish the facts, like how long we've been dating," he finished lamely.

"Six months?"

"How did we meet?"

"Kaitlin and Luke's wedding. But that was five years ago! Why are we dating now?"

"The timing was off, we were both in relationships, I was out of the country and now I'm back. It's easy. Why would he doubt any of it? You don't have to explain yourself to this guy, Eden."

"I know, but he stopped by today and asked me to go riding with him tomorrow at the ranch."

"You said no, right?"

She sighed and wrinkled her brow. Jon would never understand her unresolved feelings for her ex.

"Eden?"

"I said yes. I'm meeting him tomorrow at noon."

CHAPTER 6

*R*J awoke the next morning with Eden on his mind. It was the same way he'd woken every morning since loading his truck five years ago and heading south of the border on a rodeo scholarship to Sam Houston State University in Huntsville, Texas. She was his first thought in the morning and his last thought at night. She had accompanied him through four years of agribusiness classes and helped him hone his bareback riding skills as a member of the SHSU Rodeo club. But her biggest influence had been leading him to victory on the university and pro rodeo circuit. For five years, before the start of every rodeo he'd slipped her photo inside the breast pocket of his competition shirt where it pulsed against his heart and fortified his courage. She'd been his good luck charm, an angel on his shoulder, she just didn't know it.

He reached for his wallet on the bedside table and flipped it open. A cracked and tattered photo of Eden from high school smiled back. He gently stroked his thumb across her image. He was nervous about seeing her today. Their relationship had ended badly and he was solely responsible for breaking her heart. He was desperate for an amicable reconciliation today. It was his only hope because he was pretty sure asking for forgiveness would only result with a well-deserved slap across the face. His juvenile performance at the mall with Velvet the other day would probably result in another slap. RJ dropped the wallet to his chest and dug his head into the pillows. Eyes the color of a thousand summer days had haunted him since the day he'd left her behind.

It wasn't like he hadn't tried to get over her. Every rodeo had an eager supply of buckle bunnies willing to soothe and satisfy his needs, but his relationships with women never lasted more than a few months. It hadn't seemed fair leading them on with hopes of a future when dreams of Eden occupied his mind.

But meeting Velvet had changed all that. Yes, meeting Velvet Blair was a different matter altogether. She was a force to be reckoned with, as fierce and unpredictable as the horse he'd ridden on the day they'd met...

He'd misjudged setting up properly on the bronc he'd drawn at a small-town rodeo north of Houston, and when the chute flung open and the horse lunged forward, he began the desperate fight to get his spurs back to the tip of the horse's shoulders. Too late to recover control, his body snapped backwards, his head cranking hard against the horse's hindquarter. He wasn't clear on what happened next, just remembered the earth rising up to meet him before scrambling to his feet and stumbling towards the safety of the panels. It had taken all afternoon for his mind to clear but the pain had never really gone away, and the racket from the rodeo dance only aggravated his massive headache. RJ stepped from the canvas tent escaping the roar of conversation in the beer gardens and the ear-splitting music blaring from the speakers of the dance floor and wandered in the direction of his truck. It was parked along the backside of the infield, not a great distance away but far enough he had to stop and rest his head against a panel. The hard metal absorbed the pain and cooled the dull throb in his forehead. There was no way he could drive back to Huntsville tonight. He'd have to crash in his truck and head out in the morning. He closed his eyes, sucked in a breath and released it slowly.

Breathe, release, repeat, breathe, release, repeat. That's when he got cranked for the second time that day.

He heard the rumble of footsteps a mere second before their bodies collided, the force of which knocked his chin sideways and toppled his ass to the ground. Instinctively he covered his head with his forearms waiting for a second blow, but was assaulted instead with the nastiest slew of cuss words ever uttered from the lips of a woman.

RJ tried to hoist his body upwards in an attempt to help whoever was lying next to him but the waves of pain slicing through his skull kept him pinned to the ground.

"What the— You better have a good explanation for tripping me, asshole!" A series of groans was her only reply. She rose onto her hands and knees and crawled over to him. 'Geezus, hon, are you all right?'"

A brush of hair swept across his face, but he lacked the energy to sweep it away. "Not really."

"Oh sugar, I'm so sorry. I didn't see you standing there. Here." She slid an arm under his back and around his chest and helped him edge slowly into a sitting position against the rails. "Is that better? Are you okay?"

"I'll let you know in a minute." Even opening his eyes hurt. He peered blearily through tiny slits and assessed the young woman's concerned face hovering inches from his own. "What's your hurry, ma'am?"

"Ma'am?" She tossed her head and narrowed her eyes. "I'll let it go this time, cowboy, because you're hurt, but if you want to live to see another day, don't ever call me ma'am again."

"I'll never call you ma'am again." A lopsided grin tilted his mouth. "Ma'am."

"Nice try, funny guy, the name is Velvet. Where were you headed?"

"To my truck." He waved in a general direction toward the back of the arena.

"Help me out." She grasped him around the waist and carefully hauled him to his feet, assisted by his shaky grip on the rails. "Does your coach know you competed today?"

RJ shook his head, grimacing from the pain.

"Well, besides being in a heap of trouble with your coach, I think you need a doctor. Where's your truck?"

"No doctor. I've got a headache, that's all. Just take me home."

Walking to the truck proved better than anticipated. RJ's gait was steady, but slow. He emitted a moan sliding into the passenger side and flinched when Velvet slammed the door.

"Where to?" she asked, putting the truck in gear and driving it toward the highway.

"Huntsville."

"Sam Houston University?"

RJ nodded drowsily. She flicked on the signal light and accelerated, easily passing the vehicle in front of her. "Don't fall asleep on me, hon."

Barely awake, RJ heard her heavy sigh. "You ever cheat on a girlfriend, cowboy?"

"No ma'am." RJ yawned and sank his head against the headrest. It sure would be nice if she'd stop asking questions and let him sleep.

"I've had more than my share of lying, cheating son-of-a-bitch boyfriends that's for sure. The last one is still rolling in the dirt clutching his balls. At least he was when I ran you over back there. Nobody screws me over and gets away with it, nobody."

"Why would anyone cheat on a beautiful woman like you?"

A hearty chuckle broke from her lips. "Looks like I finally ran into a good-looking man with common sense. I don't remember your name, but aren't you the cowboy who took that nasty spill at the rodeo today?"

"That's me."

"Well, looks like this is your lucky day, sugar. Running into Velvet Blair is going to be the best thing that ever happened to you."

And for a while it had…

Velvet had entered his life when he was in need of a friend and a lover. She'd helped him recover from his crippling concussion, become his constant companion and rowdiest fan at his remaining college rodeos. After graduation, she'd introduced him to a lifestyle he could only dream about. He was in love with her wit, her charm and her sensuality.

He was in love with everything she had offered him, he just wasn't sure he was in love *with her*.

RJ silenced the alarm on his iPhone with a swipe of a finger, threw back the covers and swung his legs over the side of the bed. Resting his hands on his knees, he stared vacantly at the blemished floor planks of his childhood bedroom.

RJ thrust a hand through his hair and released a deep breath.

Because if he was in love with Velvet, why was he dreaming of Eden?

CHAPTER 7

"Hey girl, remember me?" Eden scratched an affectionate trail down the American Paint Horse's neck.

Polly whinnied and flipped her head high, straining against the reins tied to the hitching post. Slivers of silky, coffee-colored mane whipped Eden's shoulder. She brushed them away, dug into her purse and pulled out the apple she'd thrown in this morning. "Now do you remember me?"

The horse whinnied again and snatched the apple from her outstretched palm. "Oh sure, I'm okay now that I've bribed you with a treat." Polly curled her upper lip and fully exposed her front teeth. "Don't you laugh at me," Eden said sternly, "I brought this apple on purpose." She lovingly stroked the horse's well-muscled neck ignoring the persistent nudge for another apple. Eden chuckled. "If you're nice to me today I may have a treat for you later." She patted the horse's jaw and turned to face the heart of the ranch and the only place where she'd ever felt safe.

RJ's Auntie Rae and Uncle Harold had welcomed her into their home no questions asked and had provided temporary salvation from the abuse of an alcoholic father and emotionally absentee mother. She'd always felt more at home on the Benson ranch than anywhere in the world and feeling that serenity return was a welcome relief from the anxiety clutching at her stomach.

Seeing RJ again was a dream she'd harbored deep in a secret corner of her heart for five long years. She needed to see him. She needed closure on the past. They hadn't spoken since the day she'd caught him cheating with Brittany Hews. He'd never tried to explain his betrayal, ask her forgiveness, or even attempt to contact her to say goodbye the day he left for Texas. Every detail about the way their relationship ended was wrong. In order to finally move on with someone else, she needed answers to shake the unhealthy bond still holding them together once and for all. At least that's what she'd been telling herself all morning in the most unconvincing way.

"Eden! I thought I heard you drive in. Oh honey, it's so good to see you again!" Auntie Rae flung open the door of the farmhouse and rushed down the steps, the porch door banging behind her and the fringe of her royal-blue cardigan flying in the wind.

Arms wide, Eden sprinted forward and met her halfway, encircling her in a ferocious hug. "I've missed you, too." She pressed her head against the older woman's graying tresses and gave her an extra squeeze while memories of her youth flooded her mind.

She and Kaitlin had spent much of their teenage years with RJ at the Benson Ranch. Countless hours on horseback helping Uncle Harold herd cattle in the crisp morning air, dashing to the creek when the heat got unbearable and floating on inner tubes down the sluggish, muddy water, then ending the day stuffing themselves with hot dogs and gooey marshmallows roasted over an open fire. There was endless laughter around the scarred farmhouse table, hearty home-cooked meals to nourish their bellies after a long day on the range, and always an unconditional supply of love.

Auntie Rae pulled from her embrace and stroked the soft material of her cardigan. "How do I look? It's an Eden Blue original."

Eden smiled, tears brimming in her eyes. "I designed it with you in mind. You're beautiful, Auntie Rae."

"And look at you! I swear you get more gorgeous every time I see you." She cast Eden a critical eye and clucked her tongue. "You girls nowadays," she said, shaking her head, "all so skinny, it's like hugging a bag of bones! Hah! Well, it just so happens I have a remedy for that. Come on." She grinned, linking her arm through Eden's. "Let's go fatten you up."

～

"SAVE ANY COOKIES FOR ME?" RJ placed his hat on the kitchen counter and slid into a chair across from the two ladies. "Really, Auntie Rae?" He pointed to a bottle of cream liqueur placed in the center of the table beside a plate of chocolate chip cookies.

"Why not?" She grinned. "It's five o'clock somewhere, and besides, I'm pretty sure it says somewhere on the bottle it tastes delicious in coffee."

"I'm sure it does, but what am I going to do if Eden has too much to drink and falls off her horse?" He laughed and popped a cookie into his mouth. "Which reminds me, we should probably get going." He glanced at Eden and smiled.

"So soon? I was just getting the inside scoop on Eden's glamorous lifestyle in High River and Calgary." She sipped at her coffee. "Don't forget your lunch." She pointed to the fridge.

RJ rose, kissed her cheek and swiped another cookie from the plate. "Thank you. We should be back around five-thirty."

"Supper's at six. Don't be late."

～

THE PORCH DOOR slammed shut behind them. RJ caught Eden's pinkie with his little finger as they walked towards the hitching post over by the barn. The sorrow in her eyes matched the sadness in his

41

heart, but she didn't pull away from his touch. Was it a sign she was willing to forgive and forget? The simple heat of her skin, even if it was the mere tip of a finger, made him harden beneath his jeans. Damn. "I'm glad you came today, Edie."

"Me too, but we have a lot talk about, RJ."

"We will." He dipped his head, avoiding her eyes. "I noticed you sucking up to Polly earlier. It won't work you know, she only has eyes for me."

"We'll see about that. Hey, pretty girl, who do you like better? Me or RJ?" she called to the horse.

Polly shook her head and neighed in Eden's direction.

"What were you saying about only having eyes for you?"

RJ chuckled. "You win, but only because she thinks you have another apple. I *should* make you ride Shadow." He reached behind the saddle on the other horse, placed their lunch inside the saddlebag and flipped it closed.

"Us chickies have to stick together, don't we?" She patted Polly's neck affectionately, grabbed the reins, a handful of mane and saddle horn with her right hand and placed her left boot in the stirrup. With a quick bounce, she flung her right leg up and over the horse's back and settled squarely in the saddle.

"Not bad for a city slicker." He grinned and dipped his chin in approval.

"I didn't quit riding just because you disappeared, you know. Kaitlin and I ride at least once a week."

"What about your boyfriend? Does he ride?"

"I'm teaching him. He gets better every day."

She avoided his gaze and he wondered if she was stretching the truth about her boyfriend's skills. "We should go riding when Velvet gets back, although you're welcome to come out any time."

"I'll ask. Jon's pretty busy at work. He doesn't have much downtime."

"Right. We should get going. Uncle Harold wants me to check the cattle over by the creek before lunch." He gently squeezed his thighs against the side of the horse and Shadow moved alongside Eden and Polly. "It's gonna be a hot one today." He placed a worn and tattered cowboy hat on her head. "You always did look good in a hat." He smiled and admired the gloss of her cinnamon locks shimmering in the sun, longing to run his fingers through the silky mess.

"I remember this. It's your lucky hat. The one you wore at the first competition you won."

RJ nodded. "Auntie Rae refuses to throw it away."

"What if I lose it?"

"No worries. I have a dozen more just like it." He grinned and squeezed his knees against his horse, nudging him to move forward. "I don't keep the unlucky ones."

"Thanks." She adjusted the cowboy hat low on her forehead and smiled at him. "How do I look?"

Adorable, he thought, the same way she'd looked the last time they'd ridden down to the creek together. He exhaled sharply. Five and a half hours alone with her in the back country. What could possibility go wrong?

CHAPTER 8

*A*n arid gust of wind whipped across the dry, grassy plains lifting the coppery tips of Eden's hair as she hopped off her horse and disappeared below the creek's bank, leading to their old swimming hole.

"Just like old times, leaving me here to do all the work," RJ muttered, tying the horses to a tree and unpacking supplies for lunch.

The ride to the pasture had been relatively quiet. Framing the proper way to talk about their breakup was proving to be more difficult than he thought. The one-way conversation puttering away in his head all morning made perfectly good sense if you were willing to justify the situation. A situation he was pretty sure Eden wasn't ready to accept, not after the way he'd wounded her with his lies and actions.

The edge of the red-checked picnic blanket flapped wildly in a sudden blast of wind and snapped hard against his cheek. He rubbed at the tender spot of skin and winced. Wasn't the first slap he anticipated getting today. He flicked the blanket again and the thick cottony fabric floated smoothly to the ground.

"RJ! Hurry!"

44

What the hell? The lunch cooler he'd just removed from Shadow's saddlebag slipped from his hands and thudded against the ground. He bounded towards the creek, flew over the slippery bank and tripped on Eden's boots, landing face first in the shallow water.

"Are you all right?"

Her body quaked shakily atop the large flat rock in the middle of the creek and she doubled over, peals of laughter rolling from her lips. "You should have seen your face," she gasped, wiping tears from her cheek and erupting with laughter all over again.

"You better have a good exclamation for this," he growled, rising to his knees and wiping his dripping face. "What was so damned urgent I had to get soaking wet?"

"Oh, uh." She dabbed her eyes and coughed, covering the laughter bubbling up from her throat. "There was rustling in the bushes and I was stuck on this rock." She giggled. "And, I thought I heard a bear."

Branches cracked beneath the thick undergrowth on the opposite bank. Eden shrieked and their bodies whirled towards the clatter. A doe and her fawn, startled by their presence, darted quickly away and scurried across the creek, coating Eden and RJ in a thick spray of water.

"I got wet for a couple of deer?" He stumbled to his feet, grasped her by the waist and dragged her from the rock into the deepest part of the creek. Eden screamed and playfully resisted, giggling and tugging against the slow pull of her body into the cool languid stream. He dunked her head below the surface. She emerged sputtering and gasping for air.

"Truce," she pleaded between spurts of laughter, "I really thought it was a bear."

RJ chuckled and squeezed her in his arms. "You know it'll take a month for my boots to dry out. How am I supposed to win Stampede in wet boots, Edie?"

"I'm sorry."

He raised an eyebrow. The mischief playing in her eyes most

certainly betrayed the innocence of her voice. "I'm not so sure of that, but I accept your apology." The side of his mouth lifted in a grin. "At least for now."

Eden relaxed contentedly against his chest surrendering to the comforting beat of his heart and the reassuring safety of his arms. Streaks of midday sun poked ceremoniously between towering pine-laden boughs and they floated wordlessly into the shadows of the opposite bank and away from the sun's glaring heat.

"Mmm." Eden sighed. "This is nice."

"Like old times." The warmth of his breath spread a silken path across the cool arch of her neck and she slowly turned, wrapped her thighs around his waist and curled her dripping fingers through his soggy dark curls.

"It's not old times anymore, RJ."

"No," he murmured softly. "I guess it's not." He hadn't missed the catch in her throat or the pain clouding the blue of her eyes. Her touch was tender, her voice gentle and low. He seized the chance to catch her hands as they slipped from his hair and pressed her fingertips against his firm, moist lips. Their gaze met, held, and a surge of longing rushed through his limbs.

If only he could tell her how much he missed her, how she was his first thought in the morning and his last thought at the end of the day. How the memory of their past invaded every aspect of his life, especially and most troubling when he was in the arms of another woman. He wanted her to know they still belonged together. Overwhelmed by the ache in his heart he brought her mouth to his and kissed her warm yielding lips.

Eden wrenched back, trembling and noticeably shaken. "We can't," she whispered, her fingertips lingering on his bottom lip, "it's not right. We're in relationships with other people."

A sudden cluster of leaves shook loose from the wind-battered poplars lining the creek. They churned and danced, grazing RJ's and Eden's shoulders before being pulled by a slow moving current to the murky shallows below.

RJ lowered his eyes. "I'm sorry, I shouldn't have—"

Her fingertips silenced his apology. "The old times are gone, RJ."

They waded silently towards the shore, retrieved Eden's boots and trudged up the bank towards the shelter of the shade tree. RJ flopped against the tree trunk, tugged off his boots, whipped off his socks and wrung a small rivulet of water onto the parched ground. Unfastening his belt, he flicked open the button on his jeans, and peeled the wet, heavy denim down his legs. He was first to break the uncomfortable strain between them. "I figure if we hang everything on the tree they'll be dry after lunch. It's friggin' hot out here." He flung his jeans across a branch and raised an eyebrow at her shocked expression. "You might want to do the same unless you enjoy riding in wet jeans."

SHE COULDN'T HELP but gawk. Her heart jumped at his nakedness and she slumped to her knees, rational thought and the ability to stand apparently erased from her mind. Enormous drops of creek water dripped from the heavy wet curls on his head and spilled across his thick, perfectly sculpted chest, pooling along the ripped indentations of his abs as they trickled in a slow captivating race to the sealed band of his boxer briefs. Eden sucked in a breath and nibbled her bottom lip. This wasn't the same body she'd so tenderly caressed and made love to as a teenager. No, that was the body of a slim eighteen-year-old cowboy naturally shaped by hard work and a strenuous life on the ranch. RJ had evolved into muscular perfection, choosing Velvet Blair, of all women, to share it with.

Jealousy gnawed at Eden.

She didn't know for sure, but first impressions were rarely wrong and she assumed Velvet was as demanding and arrogant as she appeared. Five years ago, RJ wouldn't have looked twice at someone like Velvet. Back then, he had been in love with her and the life they had planned, working side by side on the ranch and building her fashion designs into a successful online business. Eden's heart ached from the memory, but her mind throbbed with questions about his infidelity, his abrupt departure to the States, and his relationship with a woman so obviously wrong for him. Was it possible RJ had changed as much in spirit as in body?

"Edie?"

"Huh?" She blinked and blindly accepted the picnic blanket from his hands.

"You can use it to cover yourself while your clothes dry."

"Do you remember your first day of high school?" Eden snatched the last chocolate chip cookie from RJ's hand and popped it in her mouth.

"Yeah." RJ smiled. "I was scared shitless."

Eden rolled onto her stomach, rested her head on crossed arms and peered up at him. "You didn't look it."

"Well, I was, until you and Kaitlin came over and introduced yourselves. Why'd you do that anyway?"

"Are you kidding? You were the new hot guy, from Seattle no less. Every girl in school had their eye on you. We wanted to make sure we got to you first."

"Why?" His brow wrinkled like he couldn't fathom their reasoning.

"Because none of those girls deserved you and, we knew if you turned out to be as cool and bad-ass as you looked, you'd have way more fun with us than anyone else."

RJ smiled. "And you were right."

"We were right, except as it turned out, we were ten times more bad-ass than you." Eden clutched the blanket covering her torso and rose to a sitting position against the tree trunk. "I saw what happened to you at the rodeo in Tulsa. Is that where you got the scar near your eye?"

"Tulsa wasn't pretty."

"How badly were you hurt?"

"That depends on your definition of hurt," he answered, sounding nonchalant. "I pulled my groin awfully bad, took almost three months for that to feel somewhat better. My knees swelled up like baseballs from smacking the ground and my face and most of my head got stomped by a big ol' stallion with a chip on his shoulder. Other than a few stitches and a hell of a headache, I think I came out okay." RJ rubbed the crescent-shaped scar near his left eye. "Can't blame the horse though, he just happened to be a better athlete than me that day."

"You amaze me, you always did. I remember you coming back to school after competing on the weekend. You were so sore you could barely walk and you never complained how much you hurt or how bad your injuries were. I don't know how you could stand it."

"Pain can be a powerful motivator if you use it as a fuel for your mind and body. Every time I get hurt now, I turn the pain into determination. It makes my desire to win even greater," he concluded with a smile in his eyes and a brief curve of his lips. "But if you want to know the truth, I'm pretty much in pain every day."

"Tulsa scared me to death. I can barely watch a clip of you ride anymore."

"Hmm, so you *have* been stalking me. I'm flattered."

"Don't be. When I watch you ride, I'm sick to my stomach waiting for you to get crushed to a pulp in the infield." She shuddered. The image of him being taken off the infield on a stretcher still haunted her. "How long have you been going out with Vulva?" The nickname she and Kaitlin had christened his girlfriend slipped out before she could stop it.

Shit! Shit! Shit! Ohhh, wait 'til she got her hands on Kaitlin.

"Did you just call her Vulva?"

Eden tucked in her bottom lip, her eyes wide and innocent. "No. I'm pretty sure I said Velvet."

He nodded but his mouth curved in a smile. "We started going out near the end of college, so I guess almost a year. What about you and—what's your boyfriend's name again?"

"Jon Frazer, Kaitlin's brother-in-law. We've been dating six months."

"Keeping it in the family, eh?"

Eden wrinkled her nose at him, shook the remaining moisture from her hair, and finger combed her damp tresses behind her ears. "What's Velvet like?"

"She's as nice as they come." His eyes slid sideways. "Oh, I know she comes across strong-willed and a little mean sometimes, but she really does have a heart of gold. Her father, Angus Blair, made a fortune in oil and gas thirty some years ago and owns one of the most successful ranches in Texas. He didn't get where he is now by playing nice. He's an Irish hard-ass and he passed those same qualities on to Velvet and her brother. She knows what she wants, that's for sure, and won't stop until she gets it."

Eden narrowed her eyes. *Did she work hard to get you, or did you just fall face first for a pretty face and got caught in her lair?*

"I think the reason Velvet and I click is because she came into my life when I desperately needed a friend."

You always had a friend, Eden silently offered, lowering her glance to hide the glimmer of tears pricking her eyes. *All you had to do was pick up the phone and call.*

CHAPTER 9

"Why did you cheat on me RJ?" Eden blurted the words before she could stop herself. And frankly, she didn't care. It was time to stop beating around the bush and start talking about the real reason they were here today.

"Uh... I was pretty drunk that night."

"No, you weren't. You had two beer tops, I was there."

He shrugged. "If it helps any, I didn't sleep with her."

"That's not what Brittany said. In fact, at one point she told everyone she was pregnant with your baby."

"I didn't sleep with Brittany."

"Why would you let me think you did? I loved you, RJ. You may not have slept with her, but I caught the two of you with your tongues down each other's throats and your hands were all over her. You were fondling her breasts like you'd never seen a pair of tits before. Call it what you want but I call it cheating, and I deserve to know why you did this to me!"

He rubbed a hand across his forehead and through his hair. "I thought it was the best way..."

"The best way to what? To break my heart? To make me a laughing stock? We planned a future together, and you lied and cheated and left without a word!" She shifted onto her knees and leaned back against her heels. "What changed, RJ? Why did you do it?"

RJ sighed and reached for her hands. "If anyone from Seattle had ever told me I'd grow up to be a bareback rider from Alberta, Canada, I would have told them they were crazy. I still can't believe it myself." He shook his head in wonder. "Remember when Uncle Harold brought home the bucking machine? You and Kaitlin were here and we all tried it. Remember?" A smile shone in his eyes. "It gave me the biggest rush I've ever felt. I could hardly wait to get on the back of a real bucking horse. When I did, it turned out I was good at it, but I never expected to continue past high school. You and the ranch were my life."

Eden pulled back her hands, clasped her arms around her knees and hugged them close to her chest. "You're avoiding the question. Tell me what happened? What made you change our dream?"

RJ knew he was in trouble even before he left the barn. Digger Blue's dark green pick-up truck was parked directly in front of the house with the door flung wide open. Shit. Digger must be in one of his rages again. RJ stopped to pet the short wiry fur of a dog bouncing eagerly towards him from the box of the pick-up. "Sorry for your luck Rocky. Your owner is one mean son-of-a-bitch." The Blue Heeler's body wiggled excitedly at his touch, his cold wet nose prodded incessantly for extra attention. RJ's mouth angled in a lopsided grin. "I wish Eden's father liked me as much as you do." Rocky whined and licked his face. RJ jerked away and wiped at the drool. "Well, I better face the music, boy, I wonder what I did to set him off this time."

The sound of anger filtered through the screen door, followed by the soothing, reasoning voice of his aunt. RJ tipped back the brim of his hat and placed his hand on the door handle, stopping briefly to gather enough courage to face Digger Blue. Thank god Eden had saved enough money from her waitressing job over the years to enroll in fashion design school in Calgary. In a few days she'd be fleeing to the safety of her cousin's apartment in the city and away from her father's fury. How she'd managed to survive all these years he'd never understand. He heaved a weary sigh and opened the door.

"Are you looking for me, Digger?" RJ framed himself in the kitchen doorway distancing himself from Eden's father and the overpowering stench of whiskey.

"If you ever go near my daughter again, I swear I'll kill you," Digger exploded, violently smacking his chair to the floor. "I should have never let her near you, you drug-infested troublemaker."

"That's enough, Blue." Uncle Harold stood and reached across the table planting his large, powerful hands on Digger's shoulders and shoving him down into the adjacent chair.

"You're just as bad." Digger pointed a gnarled finger at Harold and Rae. "Letting a menace from the States into your home to corrupt the morals of an innocent girl."

"Oh, for heaven's sake! RJ has been here for three years! He's my sister's son. He's never given us or anyone else a lick of trouble. As for rumors about RJ using drugs when he first came here, they were just that, rumors!"

"You think this boy's a saint? Well, let me tell you, I caught him forcing my daughter to have sex with him—"

"You're crazy, old man." RJ started towards him, eyes blazing with anger, fists clenched for a fight.

"Stay where you are, son." Uncle Harold stepped quickly and stopped him near the door.

"They're not children, Digger, they're eighteen-year-old adults who happen to be in love. I'm sure what you saw, if you saw anything," Auntie Rae pronounced coldly, "was consensual. Now…" she pressed her palms against the kitchen table and rose, her small trim body looming impossibly large, "…get out of our home, and off our property. You're not welcome here."

"I'm not finished with you." He slammed RJ against the doorframe on his way past. "Just try and come by the house sometime,

you'll get what's comin' to you, you little bastard. Just try it. You'll see."

"Get the hell out of here." Uncle Harold shoved him out the door.

Digger stumbled across the porch, slid off the top step and toppled to the ground below. Laughter rumbled deep in his chest and convulsed up his throat. He made no effort to get up and no one rushed down the steps to see if he was all right.

"I could sue, you know," he said to no one in particular. He rolled onto his side and propped himself up on one arm, pulled a cigarette from the pack in his shirt pocket and lit it, inhaling deeply. Pillars of smoke rushed from his nostrils and curled around his head. Wordlessly he continued to smoke, calmly scrutinizing the stony faces of RJ and his aunt and uncle glowering down at him from the top of the steps. The tip of his cigarette glowed between nicotine-stained fingers as he took a final drag and flicked the butt to the side. Working his tongue over his teeth, he snorted up a wad of phlegm and sprayed the flowerbed with a coat of spit.

"You people make me sick."

With a shake of his head, he picked himself off the ground and climbed in his truck. A look of evil danced in his eyes and along the curve of his mouth. "I'll be watching you, RJ." He pointed at his eyes, reversed his truck, slammed the gearshift into drive and tore down the laneway leaving a cloud of dust in his wake.

RJ shakily plunked his elbows on the kitchen table and cupped his head in his hands. "I don't know what to do." He lifted his head, his eyes round in panic, "What if he hurts Eden?" The wooden chair legs scraped along the floor. "I have to warn her."

"Sit down, son, we need to talk." Auntie Rae gently pushed him to the seat of the chair. "Where's Eden right now?"

"In the city with Kaitlin."

"Then she's safe. You can phone her later."

"What if he goes there? I've gotta warn her!"

"The only place Digger's going is to the bar so he can brag to all *his drinking buddies about how he intimidated his daughter's boyfriend."*

RJ shook his head. "He's been crazy lately and he's always drunk. Eden told me yesterday she's scared when she leaves for school he'll hurt her mom." His brow furrowed. "I'm scared for Eden. Do you think he'll try anything?"

"As of this moment, RJ, your uncle and I are more concerned about your safety. He threatened you, not Eden."

"He threatened us all, Auntie Rae."

"He did, but you were his main target. How serious is your relationship with Eden?" She grinned at his gaping mouth and raised eyebrows. "We already know the two of you are having sex, RJ. It's no big secret. I just hope you're using protection."

"Yes, ma'am." He rubbed at the uncomfortable heat rising up his neck. "What's having sex with Eden got to do with anything?"

"Everything according to Digger. Did he catch you two having sex?"

"Kinda, we weren't exactly—you know." He shifted his eyes to the table and squirmed uncomfortably in his chair. "He was mad and threw me out of the house, but I didn't expect him to show up at the ranch and threaten us."

"Did he harm Eden after you left?"

"No, but he was mad and told Eden she wasn't allowed to see me anymore. We've been careful not to let him see us together."

"We've been meaning to talk to you about Eden for a while now and seeing as what just happened with Digger, I think it's time." Uncle Harold slid into a chair and helped himself to a cup of coffee from the tray Auntie Rae placed on the table. "How do I put this," he said, pouring a generous amount of cream into the piping hot liquid and blending it noisily with the spoon. "Well, your aunt and I think you're too young to be in such a serious relationship." He slurped at his coffee and glanced at RJ over the rim of his cup. "In a few days, Eden will be moving to Calgary. Her whole life is going to revolve

around school, studying and working part time; she won't have much time to spend with you."

"But—"

"Let me finish, son. We like Eden, you know that and if the two of you end up married, well, we couldn't be happier, but here's the thing. You're eighteen years old. You're too young to stay cooped up on the ranch with your aunt and me, fiddling four years of your life away waiting for your girlfriend to finish school."

"Eden and I have talked about it. We have everything figured out."

"You think you do. But what if Eden meets someone else? Someone she has more in common with than you. Then what? You've wasted four years of your life when you could have been enjoying new experiences of your own."

"And how would I do that?" He flung a spoon, skipping it across the table. "Are you kicking me out?"

"Help me out here, Rae," Uncle Harold floundered.

"We aren't kicking you out, RJ, only suggesting a compromise." She pushed an overstuffed file folder across the table. "Your uncle and I have always wanted you to get a proper education, and this is the only way we can help you get one. Now, we've talked with your grandfather and he's agreed to help out."

If they were talking to his grandpa, they must be trying to send him back to Seattle. Well, they could talk all they wanted. He wasn't leaving Eden.

Auntie Rae nodded towards the envelope. "Open it."

RJ flipped back the folder and frowned. Sam Houston State University in Huntsville, Texas? What was this all about?

"When we were down in New Mexico at the High School Rodeo Finals, we were approached by several university rodeo coaches, you know that. We were quite impressed with the fellow from Sam Houston and kept his card and information on file, just in case. Sam Houston has a wonderful reputation, RJ, and," she said, her face

flushing with excitement, "you've been accepted! We just got confirmation a few days ago."

"Accepted into what exactly?"

"Well, you'll graduate with a Bachelor of Science and a major in Agricultural Business, plus, you've received a full scholarship! Isn't it exciting! You can earn a degree and continue to compete. We're so proud of you, honey."

"And you didn't think I should be consulted about this?" He leaned back in his chair and crossed his arms over his chest.

"In the beginning, of course we did, but you've been so wrapped up with Eden lately we worried you wouldn't consider it."

"So how did I miraculously get admitted to this fine college?"

"We contacted the rodeo coach and filled out the information he sent us. We only want the best for you, RJ."

He ignored her outstretched arms. "You have no right to plan my life." He pushed back his chair and stood. "Sorry to disappoint you, but I'm not leaving."

"If you really want to save Eden from her father, the best thing you could do is leave town, son."

RJ stopped abruptly at the doorway and angrily whirled to face his uncle.

"Eden needs a chance to breathe without fear her father is going to harm you. She's worked hard to get into school and if you really want her to succeed, you need to let her go. She'll have enough on her plate without you in the mix."

Auntie Rae cocked an eyebrow. "It doesn't have to be forever," she said softly, "If you and Eden are meant to be, you'll find your way back to each other when the time is right."

RJ squinted towards the creek bank, wishing today was the right time to tell Eden how much he still loved her. But it wasn't. There were too many obstacles in their paths right now; his relationship with Velvet, her relationship with Jon and the incredible pressure and expectations he'd placed on himself to perform well at

Stampede. He wasn't sure he'd ever have the courage to tell Eden about her father's visit and his aunt and uncle's interference in their relationship. It was obvious she'd moved on without him. Her clothing designs were taking off, she had steady employment at Kaitlin's Western store *and* she had Jon and there was no way he'd destroy everything she'd worked so hard to overcome, ever again.

He dipped his head. "I thought it was time we broke up." His voice cracked and faltered. "I thought if you caught me cheating on you, you'd think so, too."

"That's it? You thought it was time to breakup? So why didn't you tell me that instead of cheating on me?"

"I was leaving the next day for Texas. I didn't think you'd understand? This way it would be a clean break."

"What? You never told me you were leaving in the first place, how could I possibly understand?" Eden rose to her feet and snatched her clothes from the branches of the tree, "And for your information, our break-up was anything but clean. You practically destroyed me. You're lying, RJ, I don't know why you won't tell me the truth, but I'm done wondering, I don't need the misery anymore."

RJ silently watched Eden untie Polly from the tree, hop on her back and trot away, an unbearable sense of loss ripping through his gut and tearing at his heart.

CHAPTER 10

"Why did you wait so long to call me?" Kaitlin demanded. Eden's blotchy tear-stained face greeted her at the door of her apartment. "Oh, hon." Kaitlin wrapped her in her arms and limped her over to the well-worn yellow velour loveseat. "The only thing I heard wailing through the phone was you crying *RJ*— other than that I couldn't understand a word you said. What did shit-head do now?"

Eden sniffed sadly and wiped at the tears spilling down her cheeks. "He broke up with me."

"Uh, you weren't going out, how could you break up?"

Eden sighed sadly. "You know what, you're right."

"About breaking up with RJ?"

"About RJ being a shit-head." Eden smiled weakly through her tears. "I'm glad you're here."

Kaitlin hugged her tightly. "I will always be here for you. Tell me what RJ said?"

"More like what he did." She lifted her head from Kaitlin's shoulder and plunked it against the back of the loveseat. "He tried to make out with me at the creek and I almost let him. He kissed me, Kait. It was so… unbelievably good. It took my breath away. I almost got sucked in."

"But you didn't."

"No, but it took it everything I had to push him away. I was so confused. I mean, he's got a girlfriend and he thinks I'm in love with Jon, I don't know what he was thinking."

"What a slime-ball. If I had been there, I would have kicked his ass clear out of Canada," she grunted angrily. "Tell me what happened? What did you do?"

"Long story short, I asked him why he cheated on me and he told me he thought it was time we broke up and cheating on me was the cleanest way to do it."

"Huh? That doesn't make sense. Why wouldn't he just break up with you?"

"That's what I thought. I don't believe he's telling the truth. Why would he invent such a childish plan to hurt me and then drag another woman down with him? I mean Brittany was a bitch, but she didn't deserve to be used like that. And to top it off, why wouldn't he tell me he applied for college in Houston and was leaving the next day? The whole story doesn't make sense."

"No, it doesn't. I guess we didn't know RJ as well as we thought we did. What a coward." Kaitlin smoothed a comforting path down the coppery strands of Eden's hair. "You should have called me sooner."

"Trust me, it was better you weren't here. I was so mad. Look at what I did with my bolts of fabric. I still haven't finished picking up the spools of thread I chucked." Eden sighed and gazed appreciatively at her cousin. "Thanks for coming."

"You're my best friend. I love you, Eden, and no matter how many more times you let RJ stomp all over your heart, I'll be here."

"I think I'm done with the stomping."

"Do you think you're done or do you know?"

"I'm done, I think." Her eyes crinkled in amusement at the look of disgust on Kaitlin's face. "I'm done. I'm kidding."

"You better be. Now…" she said, smoothing her hands down the side of Eden's face and letting them rest on her shoulders, "…what can I do to cheer you up?"

"We are two hot babes." Eden and Kaitlin skipped and bounced a boisterous two-step out the bathroom and in and around the other two rooms of Eden's tiny apartment. A loud thump on the floor from the apartment below only urged them to increase their unruly tempo. They collapsed several moments later in a fit of laughter, sprawled across the width of Eden's bed.

"We should invite your neighbor up for a dance," Kaitlin wheezed, slapping a hand on her heaving chest, gasping for air.

"Not gonna happen, have you looked at yourself?"

"I look fabulous."

"You look like 'Shrek'."

Kaitlin reached a hand towards her cousin and patted her cracked, greenish-gray facial mask. "We both look like 'Shrek'."

"So does my neighbor," Eden deadpanned and they both snorted with laughter. "We have to stop." She panted, clutching her belly. "My stomach hurts. Stop it." She punched Kaitlin in the arm. "Stop laughing!"

"Okay, okay, give me a minute." She gingerly wiped at the tears streaking down her masked cheeks and smeared Eden's neck with a blob of green goo.

"Gross!" Eden wiped at her neck and fluttered her olive-stained fingers. "Apart from these, I feel so much better. Thanks for cheering me up."

"I had to think of something. You're supposed to be going for supper with Jon tonight."

"Oh that. I'm not doing the fake-boyfriend thing anymore."

"What? You have to. You have to show RJ you've moved on without him and that he's been replaced by the perfect man."

"I don't know." A dejected sigh escaped her lips. "It doesn't seem important anymore."

"Are you kidding? It's more important than ever. Eden, you've got to show RJ what he's missed by breaking up with you. By the time you and Jon are finished with him, he'll be weeping in his beer and hightailing it back to Texas." The blue of her eyes sparkled in contrast to the bumpy toad-muck covering her face. She raised herself up on one elbow. "Where's my totally hot brother-in-law taking you tonight?"

"Does Luke know about this?"

"About what?"

"About your secret crush on his older, droolworthy brother."

"Oh please, he's not as hot as Luke, but you have to agree, Jon *is* gorgeous."

"He's gorgeous but, I don't know, he's not rugged like—"

"Like RJ?"

Eden's mouth parted in frustration. "No, stop putting words in my mouth. I was going to say he's not rugged like Luke. I can hardly believe they're brothers."

"So, where's he taking you?"

"I'm not sure, I'll find out when I get there."

"Jon's not picking you up?"

"He has to work late. I'm meeting him at his place."

"Ooo, now this has possibilities." Kaitlin waggled her eyebrows suggestively.

"Excuse me. I'm not spending the night. I'm coming back here."

"But—"

"But nothing. He's my fake boyfriend remember? We're going on a first 'fake date' so we're not awkward with each other when we have supper with RJ and Velvet. Tonight *does not* include a sleepover."

"Hmm, too bad, it wouldn't hurt you to get laid."

"Okay stop. This is your brother-in-law and I don't want to talk about this."

"Luke and I should come with you guys."

"Tonight?"

"No, argh…" Kaitlin flopped against the soft, down duvet and flung her head against the cushiony down. "When you meet with RJ, we can be your buffer."

"Not a chance. You guys will screw up and blow our cover."

"Think about it and let me know before it's too late to get a babysitter." She rolled towards Eden and grinned. "I'd give anything to watch RJ squirm."

CHAPTER 11

"*T*hanks for helping me out, Jon." Eden accepted a glass of wine and casually wandered from the kitchen into the open concept living area. "Very nice," she said, commenting on the white on white surroundings, designer punctuated with hits of black, red and gray. Two large windows, framed in inky hues, drew her attention outside to the splendor of the Calgary Tower and the sparkling cityscape below. Wow. What a view.

"If I lived here I'd never get anything done. I'd spend all my time dreaming out the window."

"I'm not here much." Jon smiled. "But when I am, I'm usually sprawled on the sofa in front of the TV snoring."

"Really?" She tapped her bottom lip thoughtfully with her finger. "What do you watch before falling asleep?"

"Is this fake dating info?"

"Absolutely."

"Anything sports. Does that qualify as a show?"

"Not really."

"How about 'CSI'? The whole series," he continued as she opened her mouth in question. "All of them, Miami, LA, or New York, *is* there a New York?"

Eden laughed. "I have no idea, pick something else."

"Then we're back to sports. What about you, what's your favorite show?"

"'Project Runway'."

"Project what way?"

"'Runway', it's a competition for fashion designers."

"Ah, got it. Do you really think we need to know this stuff about each other?"

"Can't hurt." She turned from the window and strolled to the sofa.

Jon plunked down beside her. "My favorite color is orange. Don't ask me why, I just like it. I eat steak rare, and at least three times a week. I'm allergic to pollen, horses, and my brother Luke. How's that? What else do you need to know?"

She angled towards him. "I can understand being allergic to Luke, but horses?"

His eyes crinkled in amusement. "Being allergic to horses is worse than being allergic to Luke?"

"You know it is," she said stabbing him in the chest with her index finger and laughing. "And I happen to know you are not allergic to Luke. He's your best friend."

"Do you mind if we order pizza instead of going out? You can fill me in about your ex and we can practice our two-step at the same time. I assume we'll be meeting at Ranchman's or at one of the tents on the grounds and my dance moves are a little rusty."

"Sure, sounds like fun, but are you sure you want to hear about my ex?"

"Absolutely, I need all the ammunition I can get to make this fake-boyfriend thing believable. When did he ask you to be his girlfriend?"

The corners of Eden's lips curved in remembrance. She had been as surprised as anyone when RJ had asked her to be his girlfriend.

It happened quite innocently on a Friday night when Kaitlin was out with her current boyfriend and Eden had been hanging out at the ranch for the weekend. While searching Auntie Rae's games closet in the basement for a deck of cards, they'd uncovered an old VHS player and a box of movies. Eden had volunteered to make popcorn, while RJ finished connecting the VHS player to the TV, bummed to discover the large assortment of movies were Western's ranging from the 1960s to the 1980s.

"Here goes," he said and blindly selected a movie from the box, pushed it into the slot and waited for Eden to return.

"What are we watching?" she asked, slowly descending the stairs, shoving handfuls of popcorn in her mouth.

"It's a surprise," he said with a grin, grabbing the bowl from her hands and stuffing it on the right-hand side of his body.

"Asshat." Eden lunged, landing square on his lap, securing the popcorn with both hands and rolling to the other side of the sofa. "Hah! Take that, tough boy from Seattle!"

RJ grinned. "I'm a bronc rider now, remember, I'm strong as a bull!" He lifted both arms and flexed his muscles. "Check out these guns, baby!"

"You're a wanna be," she taunted, "an itty-bitty baby bronc rider with three months of high school rodeo under your belt. Shit, I could beat you blindfolded with my hands tied behind my back."

"Any time, any place." He glowered, inching towards her, snatching the bowl from her hands and scrambling away.

"Hey, no fair!"

"Do you wanna watch a movie or not? Then get over here," he said, acknowledging the nod of her head.

Eden scooted to his side and thrust her hand towards the popcorn. "Truce."

"Truce." He pressed start on the remote and they watched the opening sequence in silence. "Who's John Wayne?"

"Seriously, you don't know who John Wayne is?"

"I'm more of a Sci-Fi guy."

"Not for long, buddy, you're in cattle country now. John Wayne is like the king of Westerns."

"Hmm."

"You're gonna love this movie."

RJ held his tongue for the first twenty minutes, and painfully watched "The Duke" as Eden called him, fake-beat the crap out of a couple of cattle rustlers. "This sucks."

"Shhh, it's the best part. Listen carefully, one of the guys in the background is going to mumble something… you can barely hear it because of the fight… listen."

He turned his head towards the TV and leaned forward. "What did he say? I didn't get it."

Eden grinned. "He just called John Wayne a lily-livered coward. Ooo, he's gonna get pummeled." She grabbed RJ by the arm and play-beat him in the chest. "Nobody calls me a lily-livered coward," she growled in her best John Wayne drawl and pretended to sucker punch him across the chin.

His head snapped to the side like he'd been clocked by her fist; he shook his head pretending to recover from the blow and slyly grasped her wrists, wrestling her to a lying position against the cushions. "And nobody, nobody," he repeated with a smile tipping the corners of his mouth, "calls me an itty-bitty baby bronc rider and gets away with it."

Her blue eyes sparkled in playful response, her mouth twitching in delight. She loved spending time with RJ. He was way more fun that the other boys in school.

"Nobody but you, that is," he continued, so softly she had to lift her head to hear him.

"I really like you, Eden."

"I like you too, RJ." She sucked in her top lip, and narrowed her eyes, consciously bracing for a slam dunk against the cushions or being tickled until her stomach ached from laughing There was no way he was going to give her a pass on the itty-bitty baby comment. "What's up, RJ?" He hadn't uttered a word or made a move since he'd told her

he liked her. Was this a trick? A pink-tinged flush had worked its way past his neck, spreading up his cheeks towards his two, very worried brown eyes.

"RJ?" No answer. Okay, now she was seriously worried. She pressed a hand against his forehead checking for fever. "Are you sick?"

"Nah," he replied shakily. "I just really like you. Edie, I was wondering," he said, his voice wavering, followed by a deep calming breath, "will you be my girlfriend?"

CHAPTER 12

"*Y*ou've still got it, Mr. Frazer," Eden teased as Jon tripped and stomped all over her feet. "How could I not remember your exceptional footwork from Kaitlin and Luke's wedding dance."

Jon grinned, wiggled his eyebrows and lowered his hand to the curve of her back. He plunged her in an unexpected dip. "Take that."

She emitted a startled shriek. Her rich, low chuckle floated up the length of his arm and pulsed against his neck as he guided her forward through the kitchen and back towards the living room.

"Very smooth, Mr. Frazer, but we should take a break. My feet can't take any more abuse."

"Water?" he asked, gesturing towards the kitchen.

"Water would be great, thanks." Eden slumped on the sofa and rubbed the sole of her left foot. "You are a very fun guy, Jon, but my feet hate you."

He caught her eye and smiled.

"Thanks." She accepted the glass of water and took several quick sips, quenching the thirst in her throat along with a strange flutter low in her belly.

"Tell me more about your ex." He sat on the far end of the sofa, his right arm stretched comfortably within reach along the cushiony top edge.

"Well first, you should know his name is RJ Stoke. He moved to his aunt and uncle's ranch from Seattle when he was fifteen, two months after his parents were killed in a car accident." Eden settled against the supple arm of the sofa and drew up her left knee, clasping her hands around it. A faint smile lifted the corners of her lips and warmed the clear blue pools of her eyes. "We'd all heard rumors about him before he actually showed up at school. He was supposed to be a real bad-ass. You know, drug addict, alcoholic, party animal, that kind of thing. Kaitlin and I were pretty excited about meeting him, but scared too, you know, just in case the rumors were true. We'd never met anyone like him. We spent hours conjuring up all kinds of romantic scenarios about RJ's mysterious life in Seattle before he actually came to school." She combed a hand across her hair and rested it behind her head. "Our big plan of attack was to get to him at school before anyone else had a chance to befriend him. Poor guy. I'm not sure he knew what hit him, I mean, you know what Kaitlin's like, right?"

"That I do." Jon's lips tipped in a grin. "So, were the rumors true?"

"Not exactly. He was trying to deal with the death of his parents, that's all. Looking back, RJ was actually a pretty shy guy, but the three of us were a good fit. Kaitin was the troublemaker. I was the peacemaker. And RJ— was the fall guy," she said, laughing. "He saved our butts so many times; anyway, that's how we met."

"So he was a good guy."

Eden shifted, crossed her legs under her and rested her arm along the top of the sofa. "Yeah, he was. We dated for three years, up until the end of high school. We had our whole life planned out. RJ was going to work with his uncle and continue to rodeo, and once I finished design school, we were getting married and taking over the ranch."

"Nice dream."

"Yeah it was, and then out of the blue, he cheated on me." She sighed, shook her head and averted her gaze from Jon's face. Suddenly the bookshelf over in the corner was extremely appealing. "He left the ranch," she continued, "and headed for Texas. Until this week, I haven't seen or heard from him in five years."

Jon frowned, his expression clearly perplexed. "Did he give you a reason? I mean, why he would cheat on you when you had all these plans for the future?"

"Until yesterday I had no idea."

"And?"

Eden wrinkled her nose, her face puckered in disgust. "He said he thought it was time for us to break up and if I caught him cheating, I'd think it was time, too."

"Wow, lame."

"That's what I thought, but he was only eighteen, it must have made sense to him at the time."

Jon stroked a consoling path of comfort across the top of her hand with his fingers. "Maybe it's time to let go of the past, Eden."

"I know. I've tried, but the men I've dated so far haven't measured up."

"But you're measuring them against someone you fell in love with five years ago. People change, Eden. He may not even be the same man you fell in love with as a teenager."

"I thought of that, too," she said, avoiding his gaze, concentrating instead on matching the tips of her fingers against the soft cushiony tips of his. "I just feel so…" Her voice caught, eyes brimming with tears as she fought to control the emotional army marching up her throat. She drew a shaky breath. Would it be wrong to just start bawling against Jon's chest?

He leaned slightly forward. "You could be dating the wrong kind of men. Ever think of that?"

"It's crossed my mind. It's not easy out there. Jon, it's hard meeting someone you want to go out with."

"Tell me about it. I haven't had a date in over a year."

"Having a fake relationship seems so much easier," she said, reacting to his puzzled reaction. "No small talk and no expectations. It's perfect. All we have to do is have fun, pretend to be in love and flaunt our perfect relationship in front of RJ and Velvet."

"So what happens after RJ leaves? You're a nice person, Eden, and I enjoy hanging out with you. Maybe we should go on a real date and see where it leads." He smiled at her slightly wary expression. "I'm not RJ. I'd never cheat on you. Trust me, I'm not that kind of guy. What do you think?"

Eden sighed. Despite what she'd told Kaitlin earlier in the day, her feelings for RJ were like an open wound that refused to heal. It was going to take a very special man to make her forget he existed. Jon was good-looking and fun. Maybe she should go out on a date with him when this was over? It'd be better than yearning for man who didn't love her.

CHAPTER 13

*R*J should have stayed the hell in bed. Instead, he was parked at the Benalto Stampede grounds, sprinting through his pre-ride prep in order to make it to the chutes in time. He'd barely had time to tape his arm properly and that was one thing he never screwed with. Aggravating an old injury or riding through a new one in Calgary wasn't on his wish list; honing his skills before hitting Stampede was, and the reason he was in Benalto in the first place. He quickly applied rosin to the rigging, confirmed the bolts in the handle were secure, and ran a brief confident check along the bind, cinch and latigo. Everything looked good. He grabbed his gear, slammed the door of the pick-up and made a dash for the chutes. Any mental preparation would have to happen on the run. Yeah. Like that was going to happen.

WHEN HIS ALARM didn't go off, he should have cancelled his plans to go to Benalto. Why hadn't Auntie Rae hollered for him to get up? She knew he and Uncle Harold needed to get an early start today if they were going to make it to the rodeo in time. He grabbed a quick shower and flew down the stairs into an empty kitchen.

"What the—?" Where was everyone? A faint murmur of voices outside the kitchen window caught his attention. Auntie Rae and Uncle Harold were mounting the porch steps covered in cow shit.

"Grab a bite, son, I'll go change and be ready in a couple of minutes," Uncle Harold quipped on his way past the kitchen door. "Throw some bread in the toaster; I'll eat in the truck."

"We had trouble with number one-fifty-two in the cattle chute this morning," Auntie Rae said, referring to a bad-tempered cow locked in the corral. "Your uncle wanted to check the nasty cut she showed up with the other day and make sure it's healing properly." Her hands splayed in front of her, indicating her soiled clothing. "Look at me, can't wait to ship that ornery cuss off to market in the fall." She pushed past RJ's angry scowl and washed her hands in the sink. "Throw a couple of apples and a few of those muffins in a cooler bag," she directed, pointing to a container on the counter, "I'll grab a thermos for the coffee."

"Why didn't you wake me up?" He was pissed about the late start and didn't appreciate being ordered around.

"Well, now," Auntie Rae said, calmly screwing the top on the filled thermos, "I didn't think I needed to. You're a big boy, RJ, and this ain't your first rodeo." She grinned, obviously pleased with the unexpected pun. "Now stop being a pussy and get a couple of go-cups from the pantry." His stunned expression raised her eyebrows and her voice. "Well, isn't that what you boys call each other at the rodeo? I wasn't born yesterday, you know. Now fetch those cups and I'll throw together a couple of sandwiches. You've still got plenty of time."

"Time my ass," he muttered, yanking open the pantry door. Pussy? Really? It was one thing when his rodeo buddies said it, but his aunt? He tugged the travel mugs off the shelf and snagged an open box of cereal in his haste. It toppled beyond his reach, spreading the entire contents across the pantry and onto the kitchen floor. "Shit!"

"What now?"

"I dumped the cereal."

"Leave it. I'll clean it up later." She handed over the cooler bag and thermos. "But I can't do much about your lousy attitude. You'll have to clean that up yourself."

"Ready?" Uncle Harold popped his head into the kitchen. "We better get going or we're gonna be late."

Ya think? The words burned on the tip of his tongue, but he knew better than to say anything. He didn't have time for another verbal scolding from Auntie Rae. Reluctantly he pressed his lips against her cheek.

"Give it your all today, RJ. You'll do fine. You always do."

THEY'D BEEN DRIVING north of Nanton for over an hour when he realized his wallet was still sitting on top of the dresser in his bedroom with his good luck charm tucked neatly inside. How the hell was he supposed to win if Eden's photo wasn't pressed up against his heart? At least one hour before every rodeo he followed the same routine: taped his arm, changed into his riding clothes, and slipped Eden's picture into the left front pocket of his shirt. And when his equipment was checked and ready, he'd usually try to find a place to meditate and clear the trash from his mind. Call it superstitious, but his rodeo routine never changed. If you broke with routine, you didn't have a chance of winning. Everyone knew it. His nostrils flared in anger and his chin tightened into a hard-tight line. Could this day get any worse?

"I'm sure glad you asked me to come along today, RJ. You and I haven't had much time to talk lately."

RJ gulped in a deep breath to steady his nerves. He'd be three quarters of the way to Benalto right now if he'd driven alone.

"What happened with cow one-fifty-two this morning?"

If anyone could turn his mood around it was Uncle Harold. He was a natural story- teller who loved to spin a good yarn and if this new anecdote followed the same long-winded path of all his other tall tales, RJ was positive the story of cow one-fifty-two would eat up at least a good half hour of the drive and help distract him from his worries.

About fifteen minutes into the ride, the story of cow one-fifty-two and his uncle's mellow tone were nothing more than a gentle hum against his ear. His mind wandered to the rodeo, still two and a half hours away, and, to the shit horse he'd drawn to ride. Captain Kirk was a hopper, but not the sweet kind that gave control of the ride over to the cowboy. No. Captain Kirk was a big mean, heavy buckskin with a mind of his own and the kind of squirrelly jumping pattern cowboys despised. Chances were he wouldn't win a dime at the rodeo today.

And times being what they were, he'd need a pot full to raise his bottom line. Something he hoped to accomplish by winning Stampede because as of yesterday he had a grand total of fifteen thousand dollars in his bank account. RJ released a slow, steady breath. Fifteen thousand dollars. His aunt and uncle would be disgusted with the way he'd thrown away his hard-earned rodeo winnings.

Life with Velvet was a first-class party, thousand-dollar shopping sprees, five-hundred-dollar dinners, and pricey trips to the Bahamas and Mexico. He had an eighty-thousand-dollar truck he could barely make the payments on each month, and a twenty-five-hundred-dollar a month apartment he rarely stayed in. Add in monthly rodeo entry fees, travel and motel expenses, and he was as close to drowning in debt as he wanted to get. He wondered, for the thousandth time, why he let Velvet take advantage of him.

The only upside to his depressing money situation, was being offered a job by Angus Blair to manage one of his ranches. Accepting the job would mean giving up a good part of his current rodeo schedule, but the money he'd make would be worth it and would bring him one step closer to saving enough money to buy Uncle Harold and Auntie Rae's ranch someday. He knew it would take him a good two years to earn enough for a down payment, five if he continued his current spending habits, but moving back to Alberta and taking over the ranch wasn't a dream he was willing to sacrifice for anyone, not even for Velvet. RJ nodded to himself. Time was on his side. He'd figure the details out when he was back in Texas.

THE CHUTE BOSS at the Benalto Stampede grounds was yelling for him to get his rigging strapped on pronto, he'd be coming out of chute number three in exactly five minutes. Injured fellow competitor and friend, Wade Wrexler, stepped in to lend a hand and help him set up. "Nothing like leaving things to the last minute, man. What happened? You're never late."

"More like what didn't happen. Who's leading?"

"Jesse Hancock, eighty-two and a half."

Within seconds RJ was surrounded by cowboys double-checking his equipment and offering an encouraging word as they waited for RJ to signal he was ready to ride. RJ climbed over the back of the chute, eased down on the rigging and proceeded to work his gloved hand into the rigging handle. Firmly in place, he flexed his fingers, tested the position and grip, and locked his hand in place.

"Don't rush, RJ, you've got time," Wade urged. "Don't push it, clear your head, and go when you're ready."

Wade's muffled advice reverberated in his ear like a freight train in slow motion. Lost in the zone, he leaned back, knees squeezed tight up against the rigging, free arm cocked high, and nodded his head in several quick short strokes indicating he was ready to go.

The gate sprang open and Captain Kirk launched, dangerously nicking the corner of the chute and dragging RJ's spurred heel down across the bronc's powerfully muscled shoulders. Unable to hold his balance, RJ propelled forward, his groin slamming into the hard curve of the rigging handle and his upper body sharply grazing the horse's crest. His performance was over before it ever began. Too late to recover anything resembling a decently scored ride, he managed to hang on and awkwardly rode out the remaining seconds. Working his hand free of the bind, RJ jumped to the ground before the pick-up man could reach him and sprinted to the panels lining the corral. He already knew his score sucked.

He should have stayed the hell in bed. His confidence going into Stampede was shot. How was he supposed to recover from this?

Feigning nonchalance, RJ raised his hat to the crowd and climbed over the corral, stepping right into the path of Jesse Hancock. "Well, if you're the kind of competition I'll be facing, Stampede should be a slam dunk."

"Don't count on it." RJ managed a lopsided smile, his eyes burning with humiliation. "Remind me of this conversation when I'm walking away with the hundred thousand and you're crying in the dust."

"You shouldn't even be here, RJ. Winning Houston and getting a bye into Stampede was a fluke and everyone knows it, and you only got invited to compete in Houston because Logan Meech didn't show and they needed a fill-in. You're out of your league here, man. You ain't got the skill and you ain't got the balls. You're a done deal." Jesse flashed his teeth and patted RJ's arm. "See ya in cow town, RJ. After today I'm looking forward, more than ever, to proving you just got lucky." He tipped his hat and ambled off down the runway.

Breathe, release, and repeat. He'd had just about enough of Jesse's bullshit comments. RJ flexed his fingers. *Breathe, release, repeat.* If he didn't have to compete in Stampede, he would have considered clocking Hancock across the face.

"He's a cocky bastard," Wade muttered, walking up behind

him. "Don't let him get to you, RJ. Hey, you should have double grabbed the moment the horse hit the chute, man. You could have got a re-ride and showed Jesse up."

"It's over and done, Wade, nothing I can do now."

"Yup, it sucks. How about we grab a beer, I'll help you drown your sorrows." Wade's mouth parted in a good-natured smile. "Because that really was a helluva bad ride, partner."

A chuckle slipped from RJ's lips. "Tell me about it. Thanks for the offer, Wade, but I think I'll go find Uncle Harold and head home. I'll catch you at Stampede."

"Sorry to waste your day, Uncle Harold, it wasn't my best performance." RJ flicked the signal light on the steering column and turned onto the highway.

"You're right, it was horrible." Uncle Harold chuckled. "Good thing I've seen you ride before or I would have thought you were still a rookie." His eyes crinkled in amusement. "I've enjoyed spending the day with you, son. Usually we only get a couple of hours of your time when you're competing up this way. We sure appreciate you taking the time to come home and stay awhile before Stampede. It's good to have you home."

"Did you hurt your back wrestling with that cow this morning?" RJ glanced away from the highway and over at his uncle. "You've been rubbing it all day."

Uncle Harold's face crinkled in a smile. "Well, she didn't do it any good, that's for sure." He grimaced and massaged the muscles just above his hip. "I don't know if I ever told you, son, but I've been struggling with rheumatoid arthritis for some time now. Apparently, it's moved into my spine."

"Why didn't you say anything? You know I would've come home to help with the ranch."

"I do know and that's why your aunt and I never said anything.

We wanted you to finish your education and live a little. You're only young once, RJ, and we wanted you to chase your passion before settling down. You've got a hell of a rodeo career going. We're proud of you, son."

"What did the doctor say? Can they do surgery or something to make it better?"

"There are a lot of options nowadays, RJ. In fact, I just started a new medication to help manage my symptoms. I'll find out in the next three months whether they're effective or not. The thing is, I'm not as young as I used to be and if this new medication works, Rae and I plan to start traveling and enjoy life while we still can. Maybe we'll head to Phoenix and relax in the sun this winter instead of struggling with a herd of ornery heifers." He sighed and gritted his teeth as though deciding on what to say next. "Your aunt is going to scold me because we were going to tell you this together, but I think now is the right time."

"What's going on?" RJ gripped the steering wheel, struggling to keep his eyes on the road, and the panic out of his voice. What other bomb was his uncle preparing to drop?

"Well, your aunt and I have decided to sell the ranch."

RJ slammed on the brakes and eased the truck to the side of the road. "What do you mean you're selling the ranch?" Swallowing hard he wiped the sweat gathering on his forehead, whipped off his cowboy hat and dropped it on the storage compartment between the seats.

"We haven't made this decision lightly, RJ. The ranch is our life, you know that; hell I was born there." He lowered his eyes and folded his hands in his lap. "With my health being what it is, we've decided it's time to leave."

"You can't!" RJ breathed in sharply, calming his voice. "Like you said, it's your life."

"It's a life I may not be able to handle much longer by myself, and if it ends up I can't walk at some point, I can't expect Rae to operate the ranch by herself. It's too much for her, RJ, you know that. It wouldn't be fair."

RJ took a deep breath, his eyes never leaving his uncle's face. "You should have told me. Nothing is more important than the two of you and the future of the ranch."

"That's why we wanted to give you first chance to buy it. We hummed and hawed at first, I mean you and Velvet seem pretty serious and from what you've told us, her family owns half of Texas." A raw chuckle escaped his lips. "Well, maybe not half." He tilted his head and smiled. "But a heck of a lot more than what we've got here." He turned to face RJ, uncertainty leaping from worried eyes. "Are you sure Velvet's the kind of woman who would consider leaving her family? If not, you'd be better off working for her father."

RJ's stomach lurched violently. "I've dreamed about coming home to the ranch and carrying on the family tradition ever since I left." Why would they think he didn't want the ranch?

"We talked about that, too. I can't afford to give you the ranch, RJ." He sighed heavily. "I wish I could, but we need the money to retire on. I want your aunt to be financially sound in case something happens to me." He reached for the thermos. "Want some?"

He poured a generous amount of coffee into both mugs, handed one to RJ and took a large gulp. "Ah, now that hits the spot, my mouth was getting dry as a fart." It was a joke, but RJ could tell his uncle was attempting to lighten the mood. "Hmm, there must be a cookie or two left in here." Conversation was stalled momentarily by the rustle of the cooler bag. "Best damn cookies in the world. Want some?" he asked, breaking the biscuit in half.

"How much are you asking?" RJ waved off the cookie and gulped at his coffee. No amount of liquid was going to quench the arid desert spreading up his throat.

"Fred Handers' place just sold down the road from us. I worked his lease backwards and figure our place should fetch around one point two five million if we put it up for auction. It's a lot of money, more than we actually need, so if you're interested we'd give you a better deal." He raised an eyebrow. "How does nine hundred and fifty thousand sound? Includes everything, house and yard, cattle, horses, equipment and land lease. The cattle and oil well leases will cover your yearly loan payments and still leave enough for you and Velvet to make a decent living. If you watch your pennies, of course. What do you think? You should have enough rodeo winnings by now to be approved for a loan."

RJ clenched his teeth. He would have enough winnings if he hadn't played the hero all year. Big truck, fancy apartment, rich girlfriend.

Stupid idiot.

His uncle was handing him the ranch on a silver platter and he didn't have the cash for a goddamn loan.

"Uh, a couple of years from now would be better timing for me. You know, I'd be financially secure by then." After saving a bundle of cash working for Velvet's father, he added to himself.

"Two years too long, son. We'd like to move into Nanton before winter hits. It'd be nice to have you in place."

"This winter?"

Uncle Harold nodded.

"You know I want the ranch, Uncle Harold, but I'll have to talk to Farm Credit first, you know, to see if I qualify. Uh, would it be all right if I looked into this after Stampede?" And figure out what to do, he muttered silently to himself.

"Of course, and I apologize for springing this on you. It's been weighing heavy on our minds since you arrived home. We love you like a son, RJ, and we'd be happier if you bought the ranch."

"Me too." He flashed a grim smile at his uncle, turned the ignition, put the truck in gear and signalled back into traffic.

Well, looks like the day just got fucking worse.

He should have stayed the hell in bed.

CHAPTER 14

*C*onversation with his aunt and uncle about selling the ranch had lasted well past midnight when they returned from Benalto. He barely touched his supper and he tried to be optimistic as they chatted about retiring and starting a new life in Nanton. When he finally dragged himself to bed, the anxiety over losing the ranch was lodged deep in his belly, nausea looming at the base of his throat. Unable to shut off the angst, he wearily rose at five a.m. and silently descended the stairs, careful to avoid the creaky step, third from the bottom.

The morning air was crisp and greeted him like a slap to the face. "This could all be yours," the barn swallows chirped accusingly, whipping expertly under the veranda and narrowly missing his head in what seemed like a targeted fly-by.

He ducked the swallow attack and grasped the closest pillar, lowering to a sitting position on the stairs and folding his arms across his knees. How was it possible, in the short time he'd lived here to fall completely in love with the ranch lifestyle?

Polly whinnied from the corral across the yard and acknowledged his presence on the veranda. She snorted and tossed her head, arrogantly demanding her morning oats. A small, tight smile tilted his lips. And how the hell did he fall in love with a horse of all things? Somehow, Polly and her bossy ways had wormed her way into his heart, just like his aunt and uncle. They were his mainstays, his grounding, and he'd almost lost that, too.

It had taken him a full year to appreciate the time, and more notably the money his aunt and uncle had spared to get him accepted at Sam Houston University. And he'd repaid their faithful once-a-week phone calls with sullen, one-word answers. They never acknowledged his rude manners, but it was easy to see now, how his crappy attitude could have permanently damaged his relationship with them and he was grateful for their patience.

Too ashamed to admit he didn't have enough cash for a down payment, he'd ardently pressed them last night to hold off selling the ranch, even offering to return home and work as a hired hand. They argued they couldn't afford his salary. Crap.

Best case scenario, he'd win day money along with the hundred-thousand-dollar payout at the Stampede and the ranch would be his. His Houston ride proved he had the talent to pull off a win. Overcoming the rising anxiety tearing at his gut and messing with his mind was something else.

Breathe, release, repeat.

The screen door closed quietly behind him.

"Coffee?" Auntie Rae pressed a cup of the steaming hot liquid into his hands and settled beside him on the top step. "Worried about competing tomorrow, RJ?"

"Just trying to gather my thoughts, Auntie Rae. Thanks for the coffee."

"You're welcome, son. I'm still annoyed your uncle told you about the ranch and I told him as much when we went to bed last night. We'd planned to talk to you when Stampede was over. You have enough on your mind without adding the ranch to the mix." She pursed her lips and shook her head in disapproval. "Sometimes that man just can't keep his mouth shut. It drives me crazy."

RJ reached his arm around her shoulders and squeezed her

close, taking comfort in the embrace. "It's all right, Auntie Rae. I just didn't expect to be running the ranch at twenty-three years old. I was hoping to come home in a couple of years, work with you and Uncle Harold and maybe build a house or get a double-wide trailer. I never once imagined you wouldn't be living out here with me."

"You mean you never imagined we wouldn't be living here with you and Velvet."

He couldn't find the words to respond. He just shrugged.

"Is everything all right between the two of you?"

"As far as I know. She's meeting me at the hotel this afternoon."

"Are you in love with Velvet, RJ?"

He turned towards her concerned look with a forced smile. "Auntie Rae, Velvet is a complicated woman. She's headstrong and determined to help make me the best man I can be. What's not to love?"

Her skeptical expression told him she didn't believe that any more than he did.

CHAPTER 15

"Thanks for shopping Frazer's." Eden waved to the young couple exiting the store. Forget Christmas, Stampede was the most wonderful time of the year. She placed her hands on her hips and line danced towards a table piled high with jeans. She stopped at the edge of the table and boogie rolled. Yeehaw! Take that security camera.

"Someone's in a good mood."

"Hey, Leon." She greeted her co-worker with a huge smile and boogie rolled towards him. "How was lunch?"

He shrugged. "Lunch was lunch. What's got you dancing all over the store?"

Eden laughed. "I have no idea. I'm just happy today. Business is good at the store and my clothing line is selling like crazy. I think Stampede brings out the best in everyone."

"Including you. Scram dancing queen, it's your turn to go for lunch."

"I browned bagged it today, I'll go eat in the office. Call me if you need a hand with anything."

Frazer's Western Wear had been busy all month and not by accident. Eden admired how hard Kaitlin worked at keeping her customers happy by opening the kiosk at the mall in Calgary every year for Stampede, posting daily blurbs on Facebook and tweeting weekly specials. And although the store was located a little more than thirty minutes south of Calgary, her city clients enjoyed making the trip to visit with Kaitlin and Eden and spend the day poking around other unique shops in the Town of High River.

Today, Kaitlin's girls were sick with colds, so Leon and Eden were holding down the fort. She sent off a quick text to see how the girls were doing, pulled her lunch from the mini fridge and logged onto Frazer's website to see if anything needed updating.

Leon's head appeared around the corner of the door. "Sorry to interrupt your lunch, but someone is asking for you."

"Male or female?" Happy visions of Jon floated in her head. Last night, their charade planning had ended up with supper and dancing at Ranchman's. Jon's two-step had progressed favorably from horrifying to horrible, but his line dancing ability? There wasn't enough time to fix that disaster. A grin tipped her lips. She hadn't enjoyed herself that much in ages, and in a man's company to boot. Her stomach still hurt from laughing at his goofy jokes and ridiculous dance moves. Jon had mentioned last night he'd be in the High River area today. She wouldn't put it past him to drop by unexpectedly if he had a chance.

"Female. Big hair. Texas drawl. There's actually three of them and they're trying on a heap of clothing, your line, too. The black-haired one asked for you." His eyebrow rose in question. "Ring a bell?"

Eden wrinkled her nose. "Mmm Hmm, it does. Thanks, I'll be out in a minute." What was the Vulvinator doing in High River? She thoughtfully sipped from a bottle of water, screwed on the cap and stood. There was only one way to find out.

∿

"Velvet. Hi. What brings you to High River and Frazer's Western Wear?"

"Eden honey, I'm so glad I found you," Velvet purred dramatically, sweeping a swath of gleaming black hair from behind her neck and across one shoulder.

Eden inwardly gagged at Velvet's syrupy tone. No matter what happened, she had to keep the conversation civil because both chairs in front of the change rooms were piled high with potential purchases.

"My friends, Margo and Justine," she said, gesturing in the direction of the rapid-fire chatter blasting from behind the dressing room doors, "are dyin' to meet you and see your designs. They just couldn't keep their hands off the clothing RJ bought for me the other day."

Eden smiled. "I'm happy they liked them."

"Not just liked them, sugar, *loved* them."

"Gawd almighty." A haze of bleached blonde perfection burst through the fitting room door. "Would ya look at this!" The woman spread her arms wide and high and swiveled her hips, the skirt of the red and black vintage-inspired dress swirling above her knees. "Have ya ever seen anything so beautiful?" She pressed her manicured fingernails into the curve of her breasts, gently stroking the feminine lace-up neckline. "And, can you believe the price!" she exclaimed. "It's outrageous! I'd pay twice this much in Houston. Velvet, is this the doll who designed this beauty?"

"Sure is. Justine, meet the designer, Eden Blue."

"Honey, I want two." She poked an index finger towards Eden. "What else you got?"

"Uh—"

"Justine, don't you dare move!" A young woman charged from the adjoining change room.

Whoa. Eden's mouth dropped. The woman was all legs, right up to the very tiny, very distressed denim skirt barely covering her hips, let alone anything else.

"What do y'all think? Does this shirt make me look fat?"

"No!" Eden gasped. "It's perfection." She'd never seen any part of her collection so stunningly displayed. "It's from my Lariat Gold collection."

Margo pulled at the split neckline and exposed her shoulder. She lifted her long golden tresses up and away from her shoulders and examined her image in the mirror. "Hey you, over at the cash register."

Leon lifted wary eyes in the direction of the women and pointed at his chest. "Yeah you," Margo confirmed. "Bring me some size eight boots, and make sure they're high on the slut scale. I want to sex things up a bit."

"If you sex up any more, you'll be naked," Velvet drawled wryly. She tossed her head and smiled at Leon who struggled towards her with several boxes of boots. "Are you capable of helping my friends while I talk to Eden alone?"

"My pleasure, ma'am."

"Do I look like your mama, honey?" Her voice was thick and warm and sprinkled with warning. "Don't ever call me ma'am again. Now," she said, turning to Eden, "where can we talk in private?"

Eden ushered Velvet into the office and gestured towards a chair. "What's up?" Of course, she knew the answer would be RJ and a warning to stay away from him. Why was Velvet jealous of her? She'd only seen RJ twice since his return, and after Stampede she'd never see him again. He'd be long gone to Texas licking Velvet's boots, or whatever else it was he was so attracted to. In fact, as soon as Velvet left, she was going to post her pre-purchased rodeo tickets for sale on StubHub. RJ would be out of her life once and for all.

Period.

"I'm sure you know all about me, hon. I travel in very exclusive circles and *I know* fashion. When I see something I like, I go after it."

"Like you did with RJ?" Shit. Shit. Shit. Why couldn't she keep her mouth shut?

"You could say I ran into RJ by accident and I very much liked what I saw." She raised a perfect eyebrow and bared her teeth arrogantly. "You're a very talented designer, Eden. I like what I see. You have a fresh, youthful eye and your clothing reflects it. If my girls out there," she said, pointing her thumb over her shoulder towards the front of the store, "can't keep their hands off of your clothing, just think what you could achieve with the right publicity and a truck load of money backing you up. I know the right people, hon, and with my connections and their expertise, you'll be famous before you know what hit you."

"And in return, what? You receive a percentage of my company or do you own it and I work for you?"

"Consider the offer for what it's worth and we can work out the details when you've had time to think about it. You won't be sorry. Eden Blue's Country Girl Couture will be huge." She stood and walked towards the door. "Oh, and by the way." Velvet paused and glanced over her shoulder, her jet-black eyes flashing with an eerie purple glow. "I almost forgot. If you do accept my offer, there is *one small* condition." She paused. "RJ will be off limits to you for good." She lifted her chin haughtily. "In other words, stay the fuck away or the deal's off."

What just happened? Eden sank against the back of her chair and stared at the empty doorway. Wow. She was expecting the part about RJ, that was a given, but after the supper planned for tonight with him and Velvet, she never expected to see him again anyway. Five years of no contact with RJ had flown by with no ill consequences, so 'never again' should be a breeze.

"Stop it, you traitor." She stared at her heaving chest, and pressed her palms against the pain ripping through her heart.

"No consequences my ass." The beat of her heart pounded back against her hands.

Eden wiped at the tears collecting on her cheeks and under her chin. Why was she crying for a man who didn't love her anymore? She was supposed to be over RJ and given the choice, why would he choose a woman coping with a struggling clothing business, an emotionally abusive alcoholic father, and five thousand dollars to her name, over a woman who had already given him the world. Fat chance, Blue, she muttered to herself, you lose.

She leaned her elbows on the table, cradled her head in her hands and shoved her fingers through her hair. A deep sigh whistled through her lips.

And now, of all people, Velvet Blair was offering *her* the world. Talk about irony.

Velvet and her friends had confirmed what she had always known in her heart but had been too afraid to believe. Her designs weren't just good. Her designs were amazing and ready for mass marketing. It was a dream she'd pursued since graduating from design school. If she accepted, the payoff could be, as Velvet suggested, huge. But at what cost? Was she ready to lose control of her company to Velvet and her investors? More importantly, was she prepared to blindly trust Velvet and risk losing everything?

"Including RJ?" her heart whispered in her veins.

"Ohhh." She whipped her cell phone from her jeans pocket. "I really need to talk this over with someone."

Kaitlin answered on the third ring. "Hey."

"What's going on, you sound awful. Did you catch the girls' cold?

"A cold I could handle. Is there a problem at the store?"

"No. You won't believe—Kaitlin, are you crying?" The faint hitch in her cousin's voice had morphed from muffled sniffles to heart-wrenching sobs. "I'm coming over." Eden pushed away from the desk and grabbed her purse. "Leon can handle things at the store."

"Don't come, you can't get sick, I need you to manage the store," Kaitlin stammered, a deep intake of breath rattling her voice.

"Kait, you're scaring me, what's going on?" She was already

halfway through the door. Whatever was going on she needed to be there to help Kaitlin through it.

"I'm, I'm— I'm pregnant," she wailed, followed by a fresh stream of sobs.

"I know, you told me last week. I thought you and Luke were happy about—"

"—with twins."

Eden sagged against the doorframe. "Why are you so upset? I thought you guys wanted another baby."

"Yes, but not twins! Geez Eden, with Luke gone so much, I barely manage to get through the day with the girls, not to mention managing the store, and Luke's leaving tomorrow for ten days." Her voice broke and she quietly sobbed into the receiver. "We found out yesterday," she continued, "Eden, I know you asked me for time off after Stampede so you can work on your designs, but honey, I need your help. Luke and I talked it over and we want you to manage the store. It'll only be a couple of years tops, maybe three, I prom-ise, and I'll pay you really well, with benefits, too. Country Girl has been keeping us in the black all year. Eden, you know that, you can even bring your sewing machine to the store and we can clear a space for your fabric and materials. Oh, I can't go through this without you, you're the only one I can trust with the business."

A fresh string of sobs pelted Eden's ear. "Kait, slow down and listen to me. I'm coming over right now. Leon can handle the store. I'll see you in twenty minutes."

She pressed the phone loosely against her chest. "Irony, you're one cruel bitch," she muttered mirthlessly and went to tell Leon he'd be in charge for the rest of the day.

CHAPTER 16

*R*J pushed the shower curtain aside and reached for a fluffy white towel from the stack provided by the hotel. He dried the water from his body and worked the towel across his head, rubbing excess moisture from his water-laden curls. Stepping out of the tub/shower combo, he pulled a fresh towel off the stack, wrapped it loosely around his hips and glanced at his phone lying on the vanity. Still no message from Velvet. Where was she? She was supposed to meet him at the hotel two hours ago. He checked his phone again to make sure he hadn't missed her call when he was in the shower. Nothing. She'd pulled stunts like this before at home, but never in a foreign country. Should he be worried or pissed off?

When they talked on the phone at lunch, she assured him she'd arrive around two pm, give or take an hour, 'because you know, she was traveling with the girls'. Well, the alarm clock on the bedside table read four pm and she still wasn't answering his calls or texts. Where the hell could she be? Meeting Eden and her boyfriend for supper tonight was important to him and she knew it. Velvet would take at least an hour to get ready, if not more, which would make them late and attract a lot of unwanted attention on arrival. He gritted his teeth and grabbed a beer from the bar fridge. He was getting tired of her crappy, careless attitude.

Flopping comfortably against the pillows piled high against the headboard of the bed, he knocked the cap off the bottle and scrolled through the guide on the TV, looking for a broadcast of the day's rodeo highlights. Casey Mason was leading in the bareback standings. RJ flicked the bottle cap towards the screen. "You'll get a run for your money starting tomorrow, Casey," he muttered with a nod of his head, "you can bet on it." He drained the cold liquid with a couple of gulps and placed the empty bottle next to his wallet on the night stand.

With nothing but the rodeo coverage on TV to occupy his thoughts, he ran a mental list of tomorrow's obligations. He was prepared, right down to his competition shirts that were pressed and hanging in the closet, ready for the next four days. With at least three hours to kill before supper; a bite to eat from room service seemed like the best option to help fill the time.

RJ picked up the phone and ordered a few appetizers from room service. Nothing much, just enough to take the edge off the angry growl in his stomach. Spasms of pain shot through his belly. He winced and closed his eyes. It wasn't hard to figure out the pain gnawing in his gut had more to do with stress than appetite. He shook a couple of acid reducer tablets from the container next to his empty beer bottle and popped them in his mouth. The news his aunt and uncle were selling the ranch had rattled more than his brain.

WHERE'D the horse come from? RJ tucked his chin to his chest and swatted at the heavy swag of horsetail brushing across his face. Where was he? Why was there a horse straddling his hips?

"RJ, wake up!"

Huh? Velvet loomed blearily above him, glossy strands of her coal black hair sweeping his cheeks. "Hey." He wiped a hand across his face, struggling to keep his eyes open. "Sorry, I must have been dreaming."

"About me, I hope."

"Yeah," he said, with a weak smile and a furrowed brow, certain she wouldn't approve of being compared to anything close to a horse's ass.

"I can always tell," she purred, "want to know how?"

"Sure." When did Velvet get here? The last thing he remembered was watching Codey Walton getting bucked off a bull and flying through the air.

"Your lips curl in the sweetest little smile." She softly traced the top curve of his lips to the corners of his mouth with her index finger. "Just like they do after we make love. I missed you, baby." She threaded her fingers through his curls and gently kissed the left corner of his mouth, followed by the right and running her slick, warm tongue along the bottom of his lower lip. "Did you miss me, too?" She skimmed her hips back and forth over his groin, creating gentle, sensual friction between the towel and his bare skin.

RJ closed his eyes and sucked in a breath. He was usually powerless when Velvet turned on the charm. She was an incredible lover and never failed to ignite him, but right now exhaustion and lack of sleep rolled through his body in restless waves. His gut hurt and his head ached and the possibility of getting an erection would be a freaking miracle. Dragging her hands from his hair, he folded her arms across his chest and flipped her on her back. He lay across her making sure his lower body was no longer in contact with hers.

"You are… very late." He smiled into her neck when Velvet squirmed playfully beneath him. She giggled as he nibbled on her earlobe. "Which makes me think you've been very, very bad."

Her breath hitched, her nipples peaking in hard mounds beneath his touch, straining upwards through the fabric of her shirt against his chest. "You know my bad is reserved for you and you alone, sugar. It's been a long three days and I'm so... ready to be bad for you."

"Mmm, I would like that very much, but," he said, his teeth gently nipping her lower lip, "room service will be here any minute and you're gonna have to wait."

Velvet stared, wide-eyed. "You're kidding right?" she snapped, a deep frown ruining the perfection of her face.

RJ grinned. "Afraid not, sugar."

"Well, room service can leave whatever you ordered outside the door until we're finished."

"I told them to let themselves in, just in case I fell asleep and didn't hear them knock." RJ pressed the palm of her hand against his lips and kissed it. "We'll have to save your bad for later."

Velvet sighed and rolled her eyes. "Humph, if there is a later."

"Babe." He rolled onto his back and pulled her close. "We've waited three days. We can wait a little longer." He kissed her cheek and smiled. "Chill. Tell me about your trip. What took you so long to get here?"

"It's Margo and Justine's fault. They loved the clothes you bought me the other day and wanted to get some, too. Your little girlfriend wasn't workin' at the mall, so we had to drive all the way to the middle of nowhere to find her."

"You went to High River to see Eden?" Velvet didn't like Eden. Why would she waste her time seeking her out? The burn in his belly was back, working its way up his throat. He had a terrible feeling about this.

"Mmhmm, and I'm glad we did. It gave me an opportunity to see what else she's designed. She has talent, RJ. I offered her a chance of a lifetime."

"What kind of chance?" He propped himself up on one elbow and leaned towards her with a furrowed brow.

"Chill, babe." She laughed. "I offered to set her up in business, not send her to the moon. Your precious little ex might have to move to Texas, though. Wouldn't that be nice having her close by?"

"Why would you do that?" He rubbed his hand across the pain searing his gut. Velvet was savvy in business just like her father. If she could foresee profit, she'd promise whatever necessary to get what she wanted, regardless of who got hurt in the process. There was no way he could trust her motivation behind the offer. Eden had suffered enough five years ago when he had pretended to cheat on her. He wasn't about to let her suffer again at the hands of his current girlfriend.

"I love fashion, RJ and that's good enough for me. She's talented and honestly, once I get her designs into the hands of professionals, she'll be famous." She shrugged her shoulders and smiled wickedly. "And I'll be rich. You know me. I never pass up an opportunity to make money."

"What did Eden say?"

"Don't you worry, hon." She patted his arm. "We didn't talk specifics or sign a contract or anything like that. I asked her to think about it, that's all." She brushed the sides of her hair with shiny red manicured fingertips and tossed her head. "Now, enough about me, tell me about your horrendous ride the other day. What happened, sugar?"

"Off day." He sank against the pillow. "I'll kick ass tomorrow." Benalto wasn't on his radar anymore. The prospect of losing the ranch loomed front and center, clouding any effort to concentrate and focus on the business at hand; winning enough day money at Stampede to make a down payment.

"Uncle Harold and Auntie Rae are thinking about selling the ranch."

Velvet rolled towards him with a radiant smile, delight lighting her eyes. "Thank heavens! What good news, RJ!"

He grasped the bed sheet and yanked himself to a sitting position against the headboard. "Good news? Are you kidding me? The ranch is my future—*our future.*"

"RJ, you can't be serious." An incredulous laugh scampered across her lips. She rose to her knees supporting herself on one hand, leaning towards him. "Honey, my father has feedlots bigger than your uncle's ranch and he just offered you the opportunity of a lifetime managing one of *our ranches* back home."

"I haven't accepted his offer. Yet."

"You can't honestly believe you have a future in Canada?" The smile dropped from her lips. "I won't live in Canada, RJ. You, *we* belong in Texas together. I can't and won't live without you."

"Velvet—" His head snapped towards a soft rap at the door and a muffled voice announcing 'room service.'

"Uh, could you let him in and give him a tip?" He reached for his wallet on the bedside table and handed it to her. "I'm not exactly dressed for company."

"This conversation isn't finished." She grabbed his wallet, hopped off the bed and opened the door. "Over there, sugar," she ordered, pointing to the far side of the king size bed. "That'll do."

"Hey." RJ raised a hand of acknowledgement to the server.

"I'm looking forward to seeing you ride tomorrow, Mr. Stoke. Everyone here at the hotel is rooting for you."

RJ smiled at the young man. "I appreciate that. Thank you. I'll do my best to make you proud."

"Thanks, hon," Velvet pulled a hundred-dollar bill from RJ's wallet. "Here's something for your time. Now if you don't mind—" She gestured towards the door with a nod of her head, shooing him along with a wave of her hand.

"You didn't have to be rude, Velvet." He frowned as she spun to face him. "And a hundred-dollar tip? What the hell was that?"

"What the hell was that? Well what the hell is this?" She flung open his wallet and whipped out the crinkled photo of Eden.

"Uh." He fumbled for an answer. "It's my good luck charm. For when I ride."

"I'm your good luck charm!" Her eyes blazed with rage, fingers poised to shred through the center of the photo. "Not your slutty ex-girlfriend!"

"You don't understand, her photo has nothing to do with you.

It's been part of my ritual since the beginning of my rodeo career, before I knew you." He leaped from the bed and dove towards her, his last chance at winning Stampede disintegrating before his eyes as she viciously shredded the photo.

Ragged chunks of Eden's charm drifted ominously to his toes.

"Superstition be damned. I'm your good luck charm now," Velvet drawled dangerously, "and don't you ever forget it."

RJ remained still, eyes glued to the scattered chunks of photo dotting the carpet. White hot anger screamed through his ears. 'Is this your dream RJ?' the tattered remnants shrieked, 'working for Angus Blair and bowing to his daughter's beck and call?'

He lifted his head slowly and studied Velvet's face as though seeing her clearly for the first time in his life. A measured grin slid across his face and the pain in his gut receded to a dull ache.

"I don't think this relationship is gonna work, Velvet."

"Why? Because I ripped up your precious little ex-girlfriend's picture?"

"No." He dropped the towel from around his hips and pulled on his briefs and a pair of jeans. He ignored her vicious, demanding twang peppering him from behind and slipped an expertly ironed cotton shirt from the hanger in the closet. "It seems to me, we don't share the same life goals." He fastened the last button and tucked the shirttail into his jeans. "You're a terrific woman, Velvet, and I don't regret one second of the time we've spent together, but it's plain to see we want different things from life. You just told me you won't live in Canada. Frankly, I can't imagine spending the rest of my life anywhere else."

He strode into the bathroom and swept his toiletries from the countertop into his empty travel tote and whipped his freshly ironed shirts from the hangers in the closet, stuffing them hastily into his duffel bag.

"There are only two things I've ever wanted." He returned to face her, placing his cowboy hat on his head and his hand on the door handle. "The first being that my parents were still alive. You would have liked them, they were great people. And the second is that someday, I'd be taking over my aunt and uncle's ranch and running it with the woman I love." He opened the door and stepped into the hallway. "You're welcome to stay here until the end of the week. I'll let the front desk staff know I'm leaving and to put any charges on my bill."

"I don't need your charity, cowboy, and besides, you can't afford the extra charges I could put on your bill." A cruel smile curved the corners of her mouth. "No one walks away from Velvet Blair and gets away with it. You'll pay for this, RJ."

"If you say so, ma'am." His brows rose in alarm and he quickly closed the door behind him, barely avoiding a collision with the beer bottle flying through the air, aimed directly at his head.

CHAPTER 17

"Don't you think we should wait for the band?"

"Absolutely not." Jon grasped Eden by the hand and pulled her out on the empty dance floor at Ranchman's Cookhouse and Dancehall. "When your ex walks in, I want him to see how much we adore each other." He grasped her by the waist and tugged her close to his swaying body. "In fact, I think we should start right now with a little public display of affection, or as the youngsters say, PDA."

"Um, no. I don't do PDA especially as we're the only ones out here and particularly since you're really not my boyfriend."

"Confess," he urged in his best Western twang, rubbing the tip of his nose against the tip of hers. "You're as turned on as I am, give me a little sugar, sugar."

"Stop. Oh stop." Eden burst out laughing. "Who are you?"

"Glad to amuse you, darlin'." He twirled her in a circle and pulled her against his chest. "It's a shame to waste good music when you dance as well as me."

"It's not just me you're amusing," she said wryly, tilting her head towards the scattering of patrons sitting at tables surrounding the dance floor.

"I'm going to ask the next waitress I see to turn up the lights so we can dazzle them with my moves."

"Okay, now I'm putting my foot down. We need to snag a table before it gets too busy in here."

"And before one of those saddles falls off the rafters," Jon said, pointing at the ceiling, "and hits me on the head."

"Trust me, they won't fall, although seriously, if it would stop you from dancing…" She grasped his hand and pulled him behind the corralled-off dance floor towards a table.

Seated on the farthest, darkest stool at the bar, RJ watched Eden's boyfriend spin and tug her around the dance floor. The poor sap couldn't two-step worth a shit, but geez Eden looked happy.

"She used to look at me that way," he mused, unhappily tipping back the bottle of beer he'd been nursing for over an hour and draining it dry.

Impatient and restless after leaving Velvet at the hotel, he'd driven to Ranchman's an hour early to wait for Eden. He sucked in a cleansing breath, relieved the pain in his gut was finally gone. The corners of his mouth lifted in a grin and he chuckled heartily, more like the pain in his butt was finally gone.

Truth be told, he hadn't been completely honest with Velvet when he told her he didn't regret a moment he'd spent with her. His regrets were long and many but mostly caused by his own hand. He'd eagerly guzzled the Kool-Aid Velvet offered, willingly bathing in it for over a year. As a result, he was paying the ultimate price: losing Eden and the ranch for good.

"I am living in country Hell," he said, quoting his fifteen-year-old self.

Jon and Eden were nose to nose now. RJ closed his eyes. He and Eden had been nose to nose at the creek, too, lip to lip actually; her delicate, familiar fragrance still nestled safely in his brain. If he breathed in deep enough her scent came alive, and he was emotionally gone. Eden soaking wet, lips parted, cheeks flushed, breasts and nipples hard and straining against his chest, a rush of sexual heat pounded through his veins.

Shit. Jon's hands were around her waist now, stroking and caressing the thin strip of skin peeking above the waist of her jeans. RJ placed his empty bottle on top of the bar, slapped a ten-dollar bill beside it and wandered in the opposite direction of the dance floor. If he wanted to be civil tonight, he better get his shit together fast.

~

"I'M SURPRISED you didn't want to meet for supper with RJ someplace quieter," Jon said.

"I'm surprised you'd never been here before last night. How are you and Luke brothers? He's so country and you're—"

"A little bit rock-n-roll?"

Her lips tipped in a grin at his silliness.

Jon reached for her hands. "Most of Luke's friends were from the country and that's where he spent his youth, hanging out on ranches, riding horses and working cattle. I, on the other hand, gravitated towards school sports, computers and math. We're complete opposites but somehow turned out to be great friends. Disappointed I'm not more like Luke?"

Eden smiled. Jon was turning out to be great fake date. "You know, some of the best country songs blend rock-n-roll in their music and lyrics, and vice versa. It makes for a great combination."

"Kind of like us."

"Or you and Luke."

"Or you and me." He leaned closer, his gray-green eyes sparkling with promise, despite the muted lighting. "Eden, I enjoy spending time with you. You're funny, you're talented, and despite what you may thing, you're incredibly beautiful. I believe we could have a future together. Once this charade is over, would you consider going on a *real* date with me?"

Wow. She hadn't expected this. But to be honest, she liked him, too. Jon was fun, lame jokes and horrible dancing aside. Why not give it a go. Her dream of getting back together with, RJ, had disappeared when he had lied to her about his past indiscretions down at the creek. Was it possible her new reality was sitting right in front of her?

"Sorry to interrupt."

Eden blinked and reluctantly tore her eyes from Jon. "RJ, hi."

"I didn't see you when I first came in so I wandered over there to wait." He waved in the direction of the impressive glass cabinets lining the wall, showcasing memorabilia from the Calgary Stampede and highlighting rodeo's finest riders from years past.

"Inspiration for tomorrow?"

RJ smiled and held out his hand to Jon. "RJ Stoke, pleased to meet you."

"Jon Frazer." He stood and gripped RJ's hand firmly. "Can't wait to see you ride this week. Eden says you're one of the best."

"Thank you, I appreciate it."

"Where's Velvet?" Eden scoured the dimly lit area around and behind him as he settled on the chair beside her.

"Uh, Velvet won't be coming. Something came up. She sends her apologies."

"Nothing bad I hope."

"Not in my books."

"Oh good, maybe we can meet up later in the week. Kaitlin can't make it either. Luke's away at work and she couldn't get a sitter." And she's pregnant and bawling her eyes out at home, she added silently. At least she was when Eden left this afternoon and where she should be right now, comforting her, not sitting in a bar wishing RJ would leave so she could go on a real date with Jon. A smile curved up into her cheeks. This was not how the evening was supposed to play out.

"I didn't know Kaitlin was coming."

"She wants to see you, RJ."

"She still scares the shit out of me."

"Me, too," Jon said with a grin, "and I'm her brother-in-law."

"Good to know I'm not alone." RJ smiled at the waitress delivering Eden's and Jon's beers to the table. "I'll have one of those, too. Put everything on my tab."

"That's not necessary, man."

"My treat."

A shrill wolf whistle sliced the clatter of the dancehall, piercing the music streaming from the sound system. Velvet stood calm and poised inside the entrance of the club calmly searching the shadowy premises. "Over here, baby!" whooped a man sitting with a group over by the bar.

Velvet brushed a hand through her hair, a stack of glittering diamond bracelets skimming towards her elbow. She tossed her head, her glossy black mane swinging in slow-mo seduction. She winked and smiled, confidently strutting past the row of gaping males in a brazen audacious path to Eden's table.

Eden gasped, her palms pressed in stunned surprise against her chest. Velvet was wearing the tobacco leather vest RJ had purchased from her at the mall. Firm, generous mounds of silky breast spilled above deep cleavage, the black fringed neckline swaying provocatively in time with the black beaded fringe on her Farrah Lucchese ankle boots. Eden's design of very short 'Daisy Dukes' cradled Velvet's slim, perfectly proportioned hips like a denim sliver as she coolly strode towards them. Holy cow, if Velvet's explosive display didn't boost the sale of her clothing line, nothing would. Eden's head was swimming with possibilities. Maybe she could persuade Velvet and her friends to model for her online catalogue. "Irony, you cruel bitch," she whispered, "you have potentially turned the Vulvinator into my biggest asset."

"Sorry I'm late, y'all." RJ rose abruptly and she leaned across the table, ignoring his stony expression and pecked him on the lips.

"Eden, lovely to see you again. Velvet Blair," she said sweetly, turning her attention to Jon and offering her hand.

"I thought you couldn't make it this evening," RJ said sharply.

"Oh sugar, I never said anything of the kind." She shifted her upper body closer toward Eden and Jon, excluding RJ. "My friends, Justine and Margo, you met them this afternoon," she said pointedly to Eden, "had a bit of a meltdown after we visited you. I had to calm them down. They'll be joining us shortly. I hope you don't mind. I always say, the more the merrier, right RJ?" She flashed a big, fake smile.

"Don't you remember when you walked out the door this afternoon, I made sure to remind you, you'd pay." She slid the beer the waitress placed on the table in front of RJ into her hand and slowly sipped the amber liquid. "I never said I wouldn't show up. You will pay for everything, RJ, you know that, right?" Her eyes glinted with dangerous amusement. "Bring another round, hon. One for my fella here, too."

She turned toward Jon. "Now, tell me about yourself, I hear you work in oil and gas, just like my daddy."

CHAPTER 18

From across the table, Velvet's animated performance simmered angrily in RJ's gut. He shifted uncomfortably, tipped back his hat and wiped at the rivulets of sweat forming on his forehead. Velvet was gunning for revenge and he was the prime target. The sneaking suspicion she planned to take Eden down with him tore at his subconscious. He had to put a stop to this before she got hurt.

"Are you okay?"

He started at the touch of Eden's hand on his forearm. "Uh, yeah. Why?"

"You're really on edge. Are things okay with you and Velvet?"

The level of concern deepening the blue of her eyes and huskily coating her voice blindly took him back to their youth when her drunken father angrily railed against him on a weekly basis, banishing him from seeing his daughter. It was the same when he returned home from a rodeo and unsuccessfully tried to mask his pain so Eden wouldn't worry. Against the odds, Eden had been good, and kind, and worried about him their entire relationship. It was apparent she was concerned for him right now. Why would she care?

He reached and slid his fingers down the length of the coppery strands framing her face and tucked them behind her ear. The molten silk of her hair threaded a blistering trail of heat straight to his heart.

"RJ?" Her fingers closed around his hand.

"Sorry, I was just thinking about tomorrow." He knew the lie was reflected in his voice.

Eden removed his hand from the side of her face and placed it on the table. "Why are you worried? You're one the best bareback riders around."

"Nerves I guess. Casey Mason's sitting in first right now with eighty-six and a half points. He'll be hard to beat."

"Casey Mason's the only thing bothering you?"

He shrugged and chuckled half-heartedly. "Maybe a few other things, too, I'm okay. Don't worry. I'll kick Casey's score right out of the arena." A chorus of hearty laughter bounced across the table. "Looks like Jon and Velvet have hit it off."

"Mmhmm." Eden wrinkled her nose at the close proximity of Velvet's breasts to Jon's chin as he bent his head lower to catch what she was saying in his ear. "RJ, would you like to dance?" She stood and grabbed his hand before he could answer and pulled him towards the dance floor.

"It's nice dancing with you again, Eden," he said as they two-stepped fluidly around the wooden floor.

"It's nice to dance with someone who can actually two-step." She grinned. "Jon tries, but he's a horrible dancer."

"Horrible dancing aside, he seems to make you happy."

Eden tilted her head and smiled. "Yeah, he does. Jon's a great guy, solid and very faithful."

"Ouch." His head jerked to the side like he'd been slapped. "Had that one coming."

"Yes, you did."

"I thought you'd forgiven me, Edie."

"Think again. However, if you friended me on Facebook, I wouldn't delete you."

"That's because you're stalking me." He twirled her in a circle and drew her back to his side, wrapping his hand around her waist, his fingers skimming the thin line of skin peeking above the waistband of her jeans. "They're playing our song, you know," he said, trying to ignore the rise of heat peeling up his arm and the painful erection straining against his jeans.

"Our song? I didn't realize we had one."

"Of course we do."

"And what's this song about?"

"If you listened to the lyrics you'd know it's about going on a date in a truck over to the creek."

"In the three years we dated, we never drove to the creek in a truck. We rode horses."

"But we went to the creek." They whirled in a circle and side-stepped in and around the crowd. "And you wore a white summer dress and drank beer."

"I've never worn a dress horseback riding."

"Hmm, well, you drank beer and we got naked." He grinned and wiggled his eyebrows. "You can't dispute that."

Eden laughed heartily. "No, RJ, I can't."

"I've missed you, Edie."

"I've missed you, too," she managed to say just before a group of rowdy dancers abruptly shoved her up against his chest. "Sorry."

RJ stopped short and wrapped his arms protectively around her waist squeezing her close. "Don't ever apologize for being in my arms." He held her gaze for a long, hot moment before she melted into the familiar curve of his shoulder, their bodies slowly swaying, oblivious to the mass of dancers crowding around them. "I never stopped loving you, Edie." Tears squeezed from below her lashes and he gently skimmed them away with his thumb. "If I had my way," he whispered tenderly, "I'd stay in your arms forever."

"Don't."

He felt her pull away, but he grabbed for her hand, pulling her back to him.

"Forever as in 'thanks for the roll in the hay, Edie, I'll catch up with you next time I'm in town and we can do it again.' I don't think so, RJ. It was your decision to cheat on me, and your decision to leave. You didn't even have the courtesy to explain your actions or tell me you were leaving. I believe your chance to stay in my arms forever expired five years ago when you ran off to Texas with your tail between your legs. You can't have it both ways," she cried angrily through her tears. "You know what? I don't even want to be your friend anymore. Consider yourself permanently deleted. Have a nice life in Texas with Velvet!"

"About that—"

She yanked herself from his grip and fled, shoving her way through the crowd.

"Eden, stop!"

Trapped by the sudden swell of line dancers spilling onto the floor, he called out again, his voice trampled by the roar of the music and his body tangled in a choreographed movement of limbs. By the time he recovered his momentum to escape, Eden was gone.

～

"Jon! We have to go—" Eden skidded to a stop on the perimeter of the dance floor in front of their table. "Jon?"

He emerged slightly dazed and disheveled from behind a glossy curtain of long, black hair, lips tinged with red, undisguised shock shadowing his eyes. "This is not what it looks like," he sputtered, trying to extricate his arm from Velvet's secure grip. She held tight and pressed her voluptuous breasts against his chest.

"Oh, it's exactly what it looks like," Velvet said, her lips curving in a sinister smirk. "The minute you left, he was all over me. Whew." She fanned her face with her free hand and ran her tongue along the top of her lips. "The people at the table over there were shoutin' for us to get a room, that's how fired-up your little friend was to get into my pants. If I wasn't here with RJ, I just might have gone for it. Your boyfriend is a fierce son-of-a-bitch, hon. Too bad you don't have what it takes to satisfy him."

"That's enough." Jon shook his arm free, but Velvet shoved him back against his chair pinning him against the wooden railing separating their table from Eden.

"You know what, Velvet, you can have him, take them both. I don't need Jon or RJ, or a bitch like you trying to tell me how to live my life *or* run my business!"

"Oh, sugar, you can't be serious. I only made an offer to save your puny little company out of pure pity and of course as a favor to RJ. You don't actually think you have talent?"

"I don't think I have talent, Velvet, I know I do. Look at what my designs have done for you. You actually look like a model. A slutty model." Eden tilted her head and shrugged. "Too bad you can't pull it off with some class."

Velvet's heaving breasts impaled Jon's floundering body. "*You will never be successful!* RJ and I will ruin you."

"You do that." Eden smiled and turned to leave. "Have fun with the Vulvinator, Jon." She smiled over her shoulder at him and walked confidently towards the door. "Because I'm outta here."

"Where's Eden?" A shimmer of coppery light flashed near the door and caught the corner of RJ's eye as he slid to a stop at the table.

"Gone, thanks to you and this bitch," Jon barked. "What's your game, man? Tag teaming to destroy your ex and laughing about it later? You're pathetic."

"What the hell did you do, Velvet?" RJ growled.

"Oh, look. There's Margo and Justine." Velvet lifted a sultry brow at Jon and winked. "If you're ever in Houston, hon, look me up, I guarantee you'll have the time of your life." She dismissed him with a wave of her hand and returned her attention to RJ. "Don't get too comfortable, sugar. If you think what happened tonight lets you off the hook and you're paid in full, think again. I'm just getting started."

CHAPTER 19

Slumped against a hard metal tailgate in the darkened parking lot, Eden lifted her tear-dampened face towards the twinkling stars and sighed. How could she have been so foolish to think Jon would turn out different than RJ, or any other man she'd gone out with? He talked a good game and she'd believed every word. Crap. She'd been ready to go on a date with him. Yet the moment she turned her back he'd been tonsil-diving with Velvet, ogling her enormous breasts and falling for her bogus Southern charm.

Men. Were. So. Stupid.

"Don't you worry," she commented to her smaller bosom, "one day Velvet's breasts will be swinging above her waistband and you'll still be perky and hard." A thin, sad smile curved the corner of her lip. Who was she kidding? Velvet would be on her third boob job by then and her own tiny buds would be spreading an inglorious path towards her armpits. She sucked in a deep breath and reached for her purse. Shit. She'd left it at the table along with her cell phone. Now what? There was no way she could return to the club and face everyone.

"Edie."

"Go away, RJ." She slowly lifted her head and glared at him. "I'm waiting for Uber."

"Then you might want your phone, you know, so you can actually contact them." He sat on the truck's bumper and placed her purse between them. "I'm sorry about tonight. I never meant to hurt you."

"Well, you did. Again." It didn't matter what he did, RJ had a knack for hurting her. Why didn't he just go away and leave her alone?

"I know and I'm sorry. I'd like to apologize for Velvet's behavior as well. I broke up with her this afternoon and she was pretty upset. She warned me I'd pay for it but I never dreamed she'd go after you, too." He tipped the front of his hat with his index finger and cocked his head. "Jon didn't cheat on you, Edie. Velvet blindsided him."

"Oh really. Big, strong Jon didn't have the strength to fight off the Vulvinator?"

"What? Who?"

"Where is Jon anyhow? Why isn't he here groveling for forgiveness, or is the bitch still gorging on his tongue?"

"Fortunately, she's already moved on and snagged her next victim." Jon stepped hesitantly from the shadows and exhaled loudly, thrusting a hand through his hair. "I hope you can forgive me, Eden. Velvet really did take me by surprise."

"I'd like to go home," Eden said, ignoring his plea, searching her purse for her cell phone.

"I'll go get my car." Jon turned to walk toward his parked vehicle.

"No. I'm not ready to be alone with you right now, Jon. RJ will take me home."

RJ's eyes widened in surprise. "You sure?"

"Yes. But don't talk to me, not one word. Got it?"

"EDIE?" RJ ventured cautiously as he turned his truck off Highway Two towards the Town of High River.

"My name's Eden. Not Ed and not Edie. It's Eden. E. d. e. n. And stop talking to me, I don't want to talk to you." She turned her back and attention to her Facebook feed.

"I don't know where you live."

"Oh. Sorry. Keep driving, I'll tell you where to turn." They drove in silence, Eden instructing only where to turn, winding him up and down the streets and asking him to stop in front of an older apartment building. "Thanks for the lift." She hopped from the truck and ran towards the building.

"Edie, wait!" He caught her elbow near the front entrance. "Can we please talk? I don't want to leave things this way."

"It's not your choice this time, RJ, and I told you, my name is Eden. Let go." She wriggled from his grip, opened the door with her key and disappeared up the stairs of the building.

Well shit. RJ climbed into the driver's seat and slammed the door. This was not how his night was supposed to turn out. A burst of light blazed momentarily from a third-floor window and was immediately snuffed by a ferocious snap of the drapes. He released a deep breath. Edie was pissed. He whipped off his hat and flipped it over on the passenger seat. He'd half hoped to be in Edie's arms right now, admittedly a sleaze ball fantasy seeing as he'd just broken up with Velvet, but there was no denying he was still in love with Eden and if she was truthful, she'd have to admit she was in love with him, too.

His chest rose and fell, a rise of heat spreading through him as he thought about the warmth of her body pressed against him, swaying in time to the music. Holding her in his arms tonight had been like coming home. He grinned. When he'd made the crack about the two of them drinking beer and being naked down by the creek, her full, luscious lips had parted in the most beautiful smile he'd ever seen. Somehow, he had to get her to talk to him and make her see they belonged together. Brow furrowed, he returned his gaze towards Eden's window. A flash of light on the passenger seat of his tuck caught his eye. RJ smiled. He knew exactly how he was going to get Edie to talk to him.

EDEN SLAMMED the door to her apartment and stalked to the window overlooking the street. His truck was still parked at the curb. "Go away!" she shouted at the pane of glass and snapped the drapes closed to shut him out. She collapsed onto the yellow velour loveseat and buried her face in her hands.

Damn you, RJ. She'd finally made peace with herself by deciding she'd be fine treating him as a friend. And what did he do? He tried to worm his way back into her life the minute he dumped Velvet. Argh! The dirty rotten, no-good, manure-stained jerk.

They were both jerks.

How could she be fooled by not one, but two guys? How could she be blind to their flaws? What was wrong with her? Tears spilled down her cheeks. She'd thought Jon was sincere when he asked her out tonight and she'd been excited about going on a real date. Jon was one of the good guys, or so she'd thought. He was gentle and kind and he'd reeled her in with his crazy sense of humor and warm seafoam eyes. Yet the moment her back was turned he was literally charming the pants off Velvet. Eden wiped the tears from her cheeks and sighed. Just as RJ had done with Brittany Hews five years ago.

Why did the men in her life cheat?

And why did she care?

Eden rested her head wearily along the back of the love seat and pressed a hand over her rapidly beating heart. The problem was she was still in love with RJ. Her traitorous heart was still doing flip flops at the fact she hadn't heard the low rumble of his diesel truck pull away from the street in front of her building. Eden sighed again.

Embraced in his arms at Ranchman's tonight, teasing her about their special memories at the creek had been a dream come true.

Eden disappeared towards the creek bank, her strong, lithe form nimbly dodging dangerous ledges and perilous gopher holes brilliantly uncovered by the glow of the moon. She covered her mouth and giggled. Poor RJ, she always left him to tie up the horses and carry the gear.

Somewhere in the distance his voice echoed through the darkness yelling at her to wait up. "You should have waited for me." He carefully picked his way down the slope, carrying a six pack of beer, a couple bags of chips and a large picnic blanket. "A bear or a cougar could be down here, what would you have done then?"

Eden laughed and pumped his chest with balled-up fists. "Oh, yeah— How would you have saved me, itty-bitty bareback rider? I would have had those critters hogtied and squealing for mercy before you even lifted a finger."

RJ raised his eyebrows. "You think so, eh? More likely they'd be smacking their lips, and groaning in satisfaction from their delicious, unexpected treat."

"I like it when you smack your lips and groan in satisfaction."

RJ dropped the blanket. "I like it when you do, too." His lips skimmed the tender skin below her chin. "Mmm, you taste good enough to eat." The creek gurgled sluggishly near their feet and a coyote howled in the distance.

Eden giggled and playfully pushed him away. "Down boy, good things come to those who wait." She picked up the blanket, snapping it towards him and laughing when he yowled from a direct blow to the butt. "Sorry," she said, but her smile betrayed her innocence.

"Let's play a game." She dropped to the blanket and sat cross-legged, facing him.

"What kind of game?"

"Strip poker."

He cautiously regarded the mischief gleaming in her eyes. "We don't have any cards."

"So we improvise... I ask a question and if you get it wrong, you take a drink." She demonstrated by sipping from the can of beer. "And then you take off a piece of clothing. Boots don't count." She tugged at her boots. "You have to take yours off, too."

"Do I get to ask questions?"

"Of course," she replied, wriggling her eyebrows, "how else will you get me naked. To be fair, I'll let you go first."

"Okay, what was the name of the horse I rode at last week's rodeo?"

"Chunky Monkey!" she whooped and pumped her fists skyward. "Yes!"

"Shit."

"Slug your beer and take off your shirt."

He eyed her warily, "I believe you said, 'if you get the question wrong you drink and disrobe.'"

"It works both ways. If the person answering the question gets it right, the person asking the question has to drink and take their clothes off."

"You're shittin' me, right?"

"Nope, that's the rules. Take your shirt off."

RJ grasped the bottom of his t-shirt and tugged it over his head. "What now?"

Eden gazed hungrily at his chest and nibbled her bottom lip. "You've got some serious muscles happening, cowboy." Her hands gingerly circled and massaged his pecs teasing his nipples into rigid, razor sharp peaks.

"FYI, Miz Blue," he said, grasping her wrists and placing her hands against the bulge beneath his zipper. "This is the only serious muscle you should be concerned with."

Eden felt a rising flush burn its way up her cheeks. "I've seen better," she boasted cheekily, pulling her hands from his crotch and backing away.

"Oh really," he said with a knowing grin, "I happen to know that's a fib."

"Maybe, maybe not. You don't know everything about me, RJ just like I don't know everything about you. Now enough about the imaginary size of your junk." Her hands shrank from an exaggerated foot down to a diminutive one inch span. "We're playing a game, remember?" She tapped her index finger against her lips. "Hmm, what should I ask you... ohhh, got it! What did Kaitlin have for supper tonight?"

"You suck. Let's see..." he mused, rubbing his chin, his face scrunched in thought, "if it's Friday, I'd say Ms. Frazer had pork chops and rice."

"Wrong! She had steak and potatoes. Take off your pants."

"How do I know you're telling the truth?" He stood and flicked the button and zipper open on his jeans and kicked the length of denim down his legs.

"You don't, you just need to get naked so I can ravish you."

He smiled, guzzled his beer and sat down. "Good point. Okay, my turn and this is a good one." He rubbed his hands together in anticipation. "You'll never guess the answer, so get ready to be naked. What was my Grandma Stoke's maiden name?"

"That's not fair."

"And asking me what Kaitlin had for supper was?"

"Hmm... you must have told me this..." She curled her tongue and slid it across the top of her teeth. "Grandma Stoke's maiden name was... Camilla Archie." Laughter bubbled up from her throat. "And when you were little, you thought your parents were calling you RJ instead of Archie and that's how you got your name. I win! Take off your boxers." She threw back her head and roared at his stunned expression.

"Who told you? I've never told anyone my name is Archie."

"I don't want to get your aunt in trouble, but she may have let it slip this afternoon when we were making supper."

"Auntie Rae and I need to talk. No one calls me Archie and I'd *appreciate it if you didn't pass this around, especially to Kaitlin. She'd make my life a living Hell."*

"I won't tell." Eden leaned forward and placed a finger over his lips, "It'll be our little secret. Now," she said, removing her finger and brushing his mouth with a sultry kiss, "take off your boxers, Archie. I'm ready to claim my prize…"

Eden wiped a fresh flow of tears from her face. Memories of their life together spilled through her mind like an open wound. What was she going to do? She still loved him, but if RJ figured he could waltz back into her life with a touch of his hand and a smile on his face like it was old times, he had another thing coming.

CHAPTER 20

"Stop buzzing me!" Eden snapped into the intercom the third time it buzzed.

"When you pulled your keys out of your purse, you left your phone on the seat of my truck," RJ blurted quickly. "Would you please let me in?"

Eden tapped her head against the wall. "Apartment 301," she answered wearily and pushed the buzzer to let him into the building. The sound of his footsteps bounding up the stairs echoed throughout the building. "Ugh, I'll get an earful about this tomorrow. Sorry, Shrek,'" she muttered towards the apartment below. "He won't be staying. I'll grab my phone, kick his sorry ass out the door and return you to your precious silence."

She cracked the door and peered into RJ's slightly wary eyes. "Hand it over." She thrust her hand through the narrow slit.

"This isn't a bank robbery, Edie."

"You are not funny." She grabbed her phone and slammed the door in his face.

RJ rapped at the door. "Edie?"

"Go away!"

He rapped again. "Edie?"

She flung open the door and scowled. "What!"

"Uh." He glanced over his shoulder into the hallway. "Can I come in?"

"No."

"Okay. Well, um, you wouldn't happen to have a spare high school photo of yourself hanging around, would you?"

Confusion lined her face. "Why?"

He shifted uncomfortably and hooked his thumbs into the back pocket of his jeans. "It's a long story, but I lost the one you gave me and it's kinda my good luck charm when I ride."

"Your good luck charm is a picture of me?" Her lips parted in surprise, the index finger on her left hand poking into her chest.

He smiled and patted his chest. "I put it in my pocket, next to my heart. It seems to bring me luck."

"Get in here." She grabbed his hand and dragged him inside.

"You have a nice place. It's not very big—"

She glanced around, trying to look at it through his eyes. It was small. There was barely enough room for the frayed yellow love seat. A small oval table was swallowed under heavy swaths of leather and suede, and bolts of colorful fabric towered perilously, adding a vivid splash to the bland surroundings. A wooden shelf jiggered between two stepladders was overflowing with bins of lace, fabric swatches and thread, and the clothing rod below it sagged beneath the weight of her designs. The cabinet holding her sewing machine was backed under the only window and a dress form was squished in the corner, her sketch pad spread across a stool. She doubted he'd understand the organized chaos within her work space.

"Yeah, it's very intimate," she replied coolly. "Want a beer?"

He slid onto the stool in front of the tiny island and removed his hat, placing it upside down on the island. "That would be nice. Thank you." She moved to the fridge, pulled a couple of bottles from the shelf and placed one in front of him.

"Still believe your luck's going to fall out of your hat if you lay it brim side down?" She sat on the stool beside him and cracked open her beer.

He nodded and grinned. "With the way things are going, I'm not taking any chances."

"As in?"

"Well, I had a really bad ride up at Benalto the other day and it didn't boost my confidence much."

"You've had bad rides before, RJ. Something else is bothering you. Is it your break-up with Velvet?"

RJ sucked in his bottom lip and exhaled sharply, "No. Breaking up with Velvet has been a long time coming." His eyes dimmed with concern and he winced when he looked at her. "She told me she'd offered to help you with your clothing line. I guess I screwed that up now."

Eden swivelled towards him, resting her elbow on the stool's high metal back. "She screwed that up herself and it has nothing to do with you."

"It has everything to do with me. We had a big fight this afternoon over… well, over many things. I didn't love her, Eden, and I hated the way she treated people. I got in way over my head when I hooked up with Velvet and believe it or not, it wasn't easy getting out. Just when I thought I'd had enough, she'd do something nice. Like last week when she talked her father into offering me a job managing one of his ranches. It paid really well, and I could use the money, but I've screwed that away, too."

"Sorry? Is that the word I should be using, RJ? I don't really know what to say. You don't seem too broken up. What's really going on?"

He dropped his gaze and peeled the label off his beer bottle. "Uncle Harold and Auntie Rae are selling the ranch."

"What?" Her lips parted in surprise. She reached out and placed a hand on his sleeve. "When did this happen?"

"Uncle Harold has health issues and doesn't think he can run the ranch anymore. They want me to buy it."

"You're going to, right?"

"I'm broke, Edie."

"But you've been winning all year on the circuit. What happened to your money?"

"I wasted it all and with what I have left, it's doubtful Farm Credit will even consider a loan."

"Have you talked to them?"

"I'll see how Stampede goes first." He shrugged, offered a grim, tight-lipped smile and drained half his beer in one gulp. "Who knows, maybe I'll win the hundred thousand." He closed his eyes and massaged the back of his neck with his hand.

Eden sipped her beer and cautiously regarded RJ's glum expression. "What happened to my picture? You carried it around for five years, how did you lose it?"

"Velvet found it and ripped it up. She was some pissed *you* were my good luck charm and she wasn't."

"And you took it to every rodeo?"

He grinned. "Since the day I left. I even took you to school with me. You're a lot smarter than I am, and I was hoping it would rub off."

"Why? Why would you do that?"

He leaned closer and reached for her hands. "Because I've loved you since the day we met. You and Kaitlin and my aunt and uncle changed my life. I screwed up and let everyone down, and now I'm losing it all over again. But the thing I regret most is hurting *you*." He gently caressed the side of her face, his eyes brimming with pain. "I won't ask for your forgiveness. I don't deserve it. I just want you to know how sorry I am I hurt you."

Eden tenderly wrapped his wrist in her hand. The hurt and vulnerability searing his eyes tore at her soul. She could almost feel a wave of forgiveness chipping away at the careful, stoic façade she'd created to protect from falling for him all over again. After all this time he still had the power to draw her like a magnet and if she wasn't careful he'd suck her in, love her and leave. She released a slow, painful breath. Somehow, she'd have to find a way to keep things friendly, even if it hurt like hell.

"I don't have another picture, RJ. My parents might have one, but I'm pretty sure you're not anxious to see my dad. I'm sorry to say he's still his old charming self. Mom isn't much better." She bit her lip and he could tell by the look in her eyes she was trying to come up with a solution. "You know," she said, jumping to the floor, "I might have something you could use in place of a photo. I'll be right back."

RJ plunked his elbows on the top of the island and dropped his head in his hands. Whatever Eden had in mind he'd try it. Hell, he'd even wear her bra under his shirt if it would bring his luck back.

"I think this might work." She handed him a painted feather. "It's supposed to bring good luck to the cowboy who wears it on his hat."

"It's beautiful." He stroked the feather admiringly. "It's got a bareback rider on it, Edie. Where did you get this?"

"A friend of mine paints them. Isn't it great? We went for lunch a few months ago and she showed me some of her designs."

He raised an eyebrow and smirked. "And you bought the one with a bareback rider on it."

"Obviously she caught me at a weak moment."

"I think the tiny little heart, up here," he said, pointing to the top of the feather, "is why you bought it. I think it reminded you of the love you once shared with a very special bareback rider."

"Are you talking about Jesse Hancock?"

His eyes widened in shock. "You and Jesse?"

Eden slapped a hand over her mouth and smiled, her eyes glinting with amusement.

"Don't do that," he said, placing his hand on his chest. "You almost gave me a heart attack. You know Jesse's an asshole."

Eden cocked her head and wrinkled her nose. "And the difference being?"

"There happens to be a big difference." His scowl changed to a grin. "I'm a nice asshole, he isn't."

"Give me the feather, I'll attach it to your hat." She took the feather from his hand, knotted the rawhide strap around the band, and placed it on his head. "Perfect." She took his hand and led him to the mirror beside the entrance. "It looks great, RJ."

"Thank you, Edie." He turned his head, admiring the feather attached to the band and smiled at her reflection in the mirror. "I feel like I have a chance again, now that I have a proper good luck charm."

"You won't be able to wear the feather close to your heart, RJ."

"You chose it with yours." He turned and placed his hands on her shoulders. "It's the same thing, Edie, maybe better."

He bent to kiss her and Eden pressed a couple of fingers against his lips to stop him. "You should probably leave. You do have a place to go tonight?"

"Yes, ma'am, I do." He tipped the brim of his hat with his thumb. "I'm staying in my friend's trailer down at the rodeo grounds."

"Good because you can't stay here." She opened the door and pushed him into the hallway.

"Will you come watch me tomorrow?"

"I haven't decided yet." Her lips pursed thoughtfully.

"I understand, but I hope you decide to come."

He quickly kissed her on the cheek before she could protest, then ambled down the stairs, his heart and step lighter than it had been in years. A lopsided grin tipped the corner of his lips. If the look in her eyes meant what he thought it did, she'd be there tomorrow, sitting in the rodeo stands cheering him to victory.

CHAPTER 21

"For the love of—" RJ flipped the comforter back, leaned over the edge of the top bunk bed and launched a pillow at Wade's head. "Jesus, Wade, wake up, you sound like a jackass humping a pig!"

Wade Wrexler groaned and peered sleepily up at RJ. "Shanna likes the way I snore. She says it's like listening to the sound of waves crashing against the shore, you know, repetitive and soothing."

RJ shook his head disparagingly. "Yeah, well, Shanna must be wearing earplugs. Where is she anyway?"

"Stayed with a friend last night. Hey, back to the subject of annoying, you were talking in your sleep last night." He laughed heartily. "Ooo, Edie. I love you, Edie. Lick my balls, Edie."

RJ threw a second pillow at Wade's head but a deep chuckle broke from his lips.

"If you're cheating on Velvet, man, you better let me know now so I can plan your funeral, because if Velvet finds out, it won't be pretty. He rose up on one elbow and stuck his head farther out of the lower bunk. "In fact, if I was you, I'd wear my protective cup everywhere I go from now on. That's the first place a scorned woman's gonna strike."

"I'm not cheatin'. We broke up."

"That explains why Velvet was hanging all over Jesse Hancock last night and you were nowhere to be seen. Must have been some shit-show, and I'm sorry I missed it. What happened?"

RJ hopped to the floor and stretched. "We disagreed about what we wanted to accomplish in our lives and where we wanted to end up. Where's the coffee?"

"Top shelf." Wade threw back the covers, sat on the edge of the bed and pushed his hands through a wave of massive bed head. RJ laughed at his friend and started spooning heaping scoops of strong, pungent grounds into the basket of the coffee maker.

"You don't happen to have an iron hanging around, do you?" RJ asked, checking through the cupboards.

"Closet, top shelf. It's not like you to be unprepared, man. I figured you'd have everything starched and ready to go."

"I left the hotel in a hurry." He pulled a crumpled mass of shirts from his bag, plugged in the iron and set Shanna's travel-sized ironing board on the counter. "See that mess?" He pointed at the rumpled pile. "That's pretty much the state of my life right now."

"Bet you're glad Velvet's gone. She really was a bitch."

RJ ran the hot flat edge of the iron down the length of a sleeve, flipped the shirt over and ran it down the other side. "It wasn't all bad." He shot Wade a quick smile. "But it wasn't all good either. And to be fair, it wasn't all her fault. She showed me a real good time but I should have gotten out a long time ago. I don't know what or who Velvet's looking for, but I sure as hell know it isn't me."

"At least you've got someone named Edie on deck or at least it sounded that way last night."

"Did I really say I wanted her to lick my balls?"

Wade smiled and handed him a steaming cup of coffee. "I

might have made that part up, but you did say you loved her. I'm gonna grab a shower and meet Shanna for breakfast. Wanna come?"

"Thanks, but I'm gonna finish up here." RJ hung a perfectly ironed shirt on the door handle, picked another from the pile and leaned against the counter. "I haven't asked, Wade, but do you miss not competing this year?"

Three months earlier, Wade had been thrown from a horse, landed on his head and neck and was still recovering from concussion-like symptoms. They'd talked a lot about it at the time. Leaving Stampede wasn't a decision Wade had made lightly. He knew better than anyone that if you weren't competing at rodeos you weren't making money and that's how he made his living. But after listening to Shanna's insistent pleas to slow down and advice from his doctors, he'd decided if he ever wanted to return to competition in top form, taking a break to heal completely was his only option.

"Yeah, I do. But hell, I'm here watching my girl kick ass in the barrel racing, and you know, sitting in the stands drinking a can of cold beer and watching you butt-heads fight it out in the arena is the best entertainment I could ask for. Don't you worry," Wade said, stopping to squeeze RJ's shoulder on his way to the shower. "I'll be back on top before you know it."

RJ JOGGED to the top row of the companion seating area reserved for family and friends on the south end of the arena, plugged his ear buds into his phone and settled back for twenty minutes of isolation. A cool midmorning breeze floated across his face and Axl Rose from Gun's N' Roses rocked 'Sweet Child O' Mine' into his ears. This was his Zen, his time to focus, time to block out the negative and breathe in the positive. *Breathe, release, repeat.*

Gentle Ben was the beast of a horse he was riding today. RJ was familiar with the big, strong stallion's bucking pattern, having been matched up a couple of times this year and with each ride, he'd been rewarded with a decent score. He mentally went through the motions of his upcoming ride, confident a positive outcome was within his reach. A blast of AC/DC's 'Highway to Hell' ripped through his Zen. He smiled and tapped his fingers against his thigh in time with the beat, a most appropriate song considering the unsettling path his life had taken since returning to Alberta.

Breathe, release, repeat. Twenty minutes gone. Time to phone his aunt and uncle and find out what time they were coming down to the grounds. He wanted to meet them at the gate and have them settled before he left to prepare for his ride. He checked his phone and sighed.

Crap. No message from Eden.

He typed a quick message. 'There's a couple extra seats by Auntie Rae and Uncle Harold if you're interested in the afternoon performance. Maybe we could get a bite to eat later. Sure hope you can make it.'

RJ gritted his teeth. It was worth a try. He pressed send and jogged back down the steps.

EDEN'S FINGERS gripped the rigid edge of her seat in the grand-stand. RJ was riding next. She closed her eyes and gulped for a breath of air. Visions of his disastrous outcome in Tulsa flashed through her mind. If something like that happened today— she should have let him know she was here as his lucky charm and, rooting for him to win. A sob caught in her voice. "Ride safe, RJ," she softly whispered. "I'm here. I'll be praying for you."

"Ladies and Gentlemen," the announcer's smooth, dulcet voice boomed across the arena to the packed crowd of enthusiastic visi-tors. "The quality of any rodeo, no matter if you're in Kennedy,

Saskatchewan— Merritt, British Columbia— or right here," his voice deepened and growled, "at The Greatest Outdoor Show on Earth…" The crowd erupted in a massive outburst of cheering and applause. He paused for a beat and chuckled into the microphone, "You've got it right, folks, YOU'RE AT THE CALGARY STAMPEDE!" The crowd roared its appreciation.

"It doesn't matter where you are," he continued, "like I said previously, large or small, the quality of any rodeo comes down to the skill of the competitors and the quality of the livestock, and I can guarantee you one and all, you won't be disappointed with the top-notch performances you're about to see today! Give a big round of applause and encouragement to the young superstars of rodeo performing for you this afternoon!"

"Now," he said, his banter turning serious and intimate. "I'm going to ask you a question and I want you to answer with a round of applause. What rodeo event do you think causes more injury to the cowboy? How many of you would say steer wrestling?" The crowd applauded lightly. "Are you sure? Because steer wrestling takes an enormous amount of strength and agility," he said cheerfully, challenging the crowd.

"All right, I can see I need to up the ante. How many of you say bull riding?" The crowd roared its approval and applauded with gusto. "And what would you say if I told you, you were wrong?" The merriment in his voice dragged across a chorus of goodhearted boos.

"Well, next to drinking a pot of strong bitter cowboy coffee that's been bubbling on the back of a campfire all day, riding bareback produces more long-term damage to the cowboy than any other event. I can see many of you out there don't believe me," he chuckled into the microphone. "Bareback riders tolerate more abuse and undergo more injuries than all other rodeo cowboys. And why is that you ask? Well, I'll tell you. For eight full seconds, the stress on the cowboy's arm absorbs most of the horse's power as it jumps and kicks and pounds into the earth below. Being atop a bucking bronco has been compared to riding a jackhammer with one hand! And let me tell you," he said, laughing sociably into the microphone, "that is a feat I for one, do not want to achieve!

"All right, it looks like it's time to get down to business. Coming up in chute one, I want you to welcome one of rodeo's rising stars." He paused dramatically. "RJ Stoke has done it all, from high school rodeo and competing in the college circuit all across the United States of America to winning the Houston Invitational and a berth at the Calgary Stampede! Now, I don't like to brag, but RJ got his start right here, just a quick hour south of Calgary in the Porcupine Hills area of a pretty little town called Nanton, Alberta.

"RJ will be trying his luck today on a big, strong stallion by the name of Gentle Ben; and let me tell you, ladies and gentlemen, there's nothing gentle about this giant of a horse! He's been a challenger in some of the biggest showdowns this season. Let's see if our man from the Porcupine Hills can prove this horse is as gentle as his name."

The chute flicked open. Eden anxiously leaned forward, her eyes wide with fear, her hands clutched tightly over the denim jeans covering her thighs. The horse and rider burst through the gate and a cry of fear ripped from her lips.

"And here we go! It's a big move out of the chute! Look at the size of that stallion! And look at him go! Watch the kick of the horse—that's gonna tell the story! Even feet—lots of air—back legs up, front legs off the ground, and RJ Stoke is matching him beat for beat. Free hand reaching *waaay* back, feet working a full spur stroke right up to the rigging! This cowboy's in a position of complete control, it's literally like watching him sit in a rocking chair sipping his afternoon tea!"

"There's the horn! Eight seconds and it's done! We have a ride, ladies and gentlemen, and what a pretty ride it was! Gentle Ben you

have met your match! Folks, give a huge round of applause for…
RJ—STOKE!"

"He did it!" Tears of joy rolled down her cheeks. Eden whooped triumphantly and leaped to her feet, smothering her seating companion in a jubilant hug.

CHAPTER 22

*R*J staggered against the sheer force of the unexpected fireball soaring into his arms and covering him in a molten splash of enthusiastic chatter.

"Oh my God, what a ride!" Eden relaxed the grip of her knees against his hips as his hands cradled below the curve of her butt. "RJ, I'm so proud of you!"

"Well, I had my lucky charm, it was a no-brainer." He grinned at the crackling energy radiating from her face. "You do know I came in second."

"It was a great ride. What'd you win? Forty-five hundred? You must be flying high right now! I was so scared watching you get ready in the chute. All I could think about was your wreck in Tulsa, but seeing you ride again in person—I mean, I watched most of it through the slits in my fingers, but," she exhaled loudly, "it was so exciting!"

The smile creasing his face spread wider at her enthusiasm. Gosh, she was pretty and so close, her breasts firm and warm against his chest, and she smelled wonderful, like the ranch's wild-flower meadow in full bloom. He breathed in deeply, inhaling the

134

essence of her beauty, her fragrance igniting the low simmer of heat flaring deep in his belly and enhancing the enormous flow of adrenaline still racing through his limbs from the thrill of his ride. Beating Gentle Ben was no match for the high he felt now with this delicious, somewhat delirious, rambling woman in his arms. Her sky-blue eyes glistened with excitement. He was helpless to do anything but smile and nod as a simmer of heat exploded. A flurry of joy and confusion popped along his veins. Oh man, he was a goner.

"It's a fantastic start and I can't wait to see you ride tomorrow!"

"If you come early enough I can get you into the stands on this side of the arena." He held his breath and hoped she'd agree.

"Oh thanks, but I paid all week for my seats over in the grandstand."

"All week, Edie? So, I was right, you are stalking me."

Eden rolled her eyes, wriggled from his arms and dropped to her feet. "Can you believe it? Jon has never been to the rodeo." Jon stepped to Eden's side and extended his hand. "I'm impressed, man, that was incredible."

"I wasn't expecting to see you today." Disappointment curved the corner of his mouth. He hadn't noticed Jon standing behind Edie when she jumped into his arms. He adjusted his hat forward to hide the tinge of annoyance he knew was clearly visible on his face.

"Yeah, well, I'd like to apologize for my behavior last night. I hope I didn't make matters worse between you and Velvet." He bent his head and smiled at Eden. "The two of us had a long talk over breakfast this morning and thrashed things out. Eden has graciously forgiven me and we've decided to give it a go—"

"—as friends," Eden said, finishing his sentence. "For now."

RJ gritted his teeth and crossed his arms over his chest. He didn't like the look twinkling in her eyes, a look she used to reserve only for him. "I'd like to apologize, too. Velvet and I broke up yesterday and she was using you to get back at me. For some reason, she felt she had to drag Edie down, too. I didn't handle things as well as I should have."

"You know what, guys? It's over and done. What are you doing for the rest of the day, RJ? Jon and I are going to go eat some disgustingly delicious food, like deep fried Oreos and Canadian Bacon Pickle Balls and then we're going to check out the midway. I'm trying to talk him into going on the reverse bungee." She nudged Jon with her elbow and chuckled. "You're such a chicken. Why don't you come with us, RJ?"

"Sounds way too dangerous for me," he said, a tease of a smile playing along his lips. "Auntie Rae and Uncle Harold are over in the VIP section visiting with friends right now. I promised to hang out and have supper with them, after that I think I'll call it a night."

"All right." Eden pecked him on the cheek and turned to leave with Jon.

He lightly touched the pleasant buzz humming against his skin. "What was that for?"

"It's a good luck kiss for tomorrow," she said breezily over her shoulder. "You've got this one, cowboy, I can feel it."

RJ WEAVED his way past the clatter and rows of slot machines lining his path. He waved at his aunt and uncle waiting for him at a table in the restaurant located in the corner of Cowboys Casino.

"Glad you were able to get a table." He dropped into the booth beside his aunt. "It's busy in here." He took off his hat and placed it brim side up on the seat beside him. "Did you win your fortune, Uncle Harold?"

"Not yet, your aunt pulled me away from the tables before I could hit it big," he complained, aiming a quick wink in her direction. "Always looking out for me, making sure I do the right thing, isn't that right, dear?" A tiny smile curved the corners of his mouth as he lowered his eyes to the menu. "Burgers look good."

Auntie Rae shook her head disapprovingly. "I'll deal with you later, Harold. How are you, RJ? You had a good ride and all, but you've seemed a little distracted all day. Is it your break-up with Velvet?" Auntie Rae gently touched the sleeve of his shirt.

"It might be rude to say, but no, it isn't Velvet. I'm sure you could both tell from the moment you met her we weren't meant to be together."

"I did wonder," Auntie Rae said. "It was hard to keep my mouth shut, but it was easy to see she didn't make you happy."

"Why didn't you say something?"

"And risk losing you all over again? Oh no." She shook her head in dismay. "The first year you were away was the hardest year of our lives. When you refused to talk to us, we thought we'd lost you forever. I never want to go through that again. You are our son." She paused. "And whoever you decide to marry is welcome in our home, even if she is a privileged, rude, immature—" she coughed, cleared her throat and measured her words carefully. "—young lady with an attitude the size of Texas."

"So, you're saying you liked her." RJ chuckled and reached for her hand. "I'll do my best to choose more wisely next time and I will apologize until the end of time for the terrible way I treated you my first year at college."

"Don't you worry, it's water under the bridge, but back to the subject of choosing wisely, how did your supper go with Eden last night?"

"Supper with Eden and her boyfriend was an eye-opening event."

"But you got along, and she did give you that beautiful hand-painted feather to bring you luck," she said, tucking a smile into the crease of her cheeks. "I bet if you played your cards right, RJ—"

"Could we please talk about something other than my love life, Auntie Rae?"

"I had an interesting conversation yesterday," Uncle Harold said. "With the real estate agent who sold Fred Handers' place a while back."

"Howdy folks, I'm Emma and I'll be your server this evening. I hope you're enjoying Stampede, can I get you some drinks before you order?"

Uncle Harold asked about the various beers on tap, and squinted uncertainly as she rattled off the options, then ordered a bottle version instead.

"Couldn't hear a damn word she said. Why do young people have to talk so fast nowadays," he muttered. "And don't tell me I need hearing aids." He glared at his wife and swept his arm across the bar in the direction of the casino. "I can't hear over all the damn noise in here."

"What did he want?" RJ asked, his fingers nervously rapping the hard surface of the table. Uncle Harold raised his eyebrows in question. "The real estate agent."

"Oh him, well, it seems there's a company from the States interested in purchasing land in our area. Fred let it slip to his realtor that Rae and I were thinking of selling, so he popped in to talk to us." Uncle Harold released a long low whistle. "I thought Fred got a helluva deal but listen, this company is offering to pay the same kind of dollars in US funds. I don't know why, but the real estate agent said they're anxious to purchase our ranch."

A twinge of dread crept into RJ's gut. "Where did you say this company was from?"

"Houston, Texas. Didn't I mention that?"

Houston, Texas, home of Angus Blair and more specifically, Velvet. The reality of what was really going on hit him like a ton of bricks. Velvet was trying to ruin him by destroying everything and everyone who was important to him. He gritted his teeth and leaned in closer as he realized his uncle was still speaking.

"So, I told him Rae and I would think it over and let him know. He's a little pushy, said the offer wouldn't stay on the table long and explained it could expire as early as the end of the week." He winked at RJ. "He was pretty keen to make the deal, but I think he's bluffing about the deadline. We don't want to be pressured into selling, and besides, we wanted to talk to you first and make sure you were serious about buying the ranch. It's yours if you want it, RJ, just say the word."

"Don't sell, I want the ranch," he said, fighting furiously against the panic flooding into his throat. "Please don't do anything until I talk to Farm Credit."

"Relieved to hear that, son, and don't worry, we won't do a thing until you get back to us. In fact, I don't mind coming along with you and answering any questions they might ask."

"Thanks," RJ said, smiling weakly at his uncle, "I'll let you know when I get an appointment." The server appeared and set their drinks on the table. Somewhere in the background his aunt and uncle were asking questions about the daily special. RJ closed his eyes, leaned his elbows on the table and sank his forehead into his hand. He could never let his aunt and uncle know the truth about his financial situation. They'd be disgusted and would probably question his ability to run the ranch. Shit. They might even sell it before he had a chance to find out if he could get a loan. Something he intended to do without his uncle's knowledge.

"Anything for you, sir?" the server asked, interrupting his thoughts.

"Uh, yeah, I'll have a cheeseburger with fries, and bring me another beer." He gritted his teeth pondering his next move, only vaguely aware of his aunt scolding his uncle on his terrible food choices and skyrocketing cholesterol levels. His gaze wandered vacantly to the TV screen. Jesse Hancock was being interviewed about today's winning ride, and Velvet, the ultimate stage candy, was clinging to his arm, hanging on his every word. Anger ripped through his brain.

Velvet.

The bitch was determined to take him down. He'd be damned if he'd let her win.

CHAPTER 23

*R*J hated to prove Eden wrong, but the final three days of Pool B hadn't gone quite as he'd planned. He'd ridden well, was happy with his performances, but he was still heading into Showdown Sunday trailing Jesse Hancock in second place.

His meeting with Farm Credit hadn't gone as planned either. The way things stood, it looked like his uncle would be required to co-sign the loan so the land could be used for collateral, the one thing RJ didn't want to happen.

Worse still, he hadn't confronted Velvet yet and time was running out for him to prove she and her father were behind the offer on the ranch.

"Don't you look lazy today. And you're all by your lonesome? Shouldn't you be whoopin' it up with your buddies?"

"Edie, hi." He rose stiffly from the lawn chair he'd been lounging in outside of Wade's trailer on the Stampede grounds. "What are you doing here?"

"It's Saturday. I don't have to work and I'm looking for a date."

"Get ditched by Jon again?" He motioned for her to sit in the chair, but she waved him off.

"Hardly." She grinned, running her tongue saucily along the

141

bottom of her teeth and wiggling her eyebrows. "I do the ditching now." She sat down on the step of the trailer and RJ settled slowly back in the lawn chair.

"You didn't answer my question. How come you're not out with your buddies?"

"I'm a little sore today, thought I'd relax in the sun, do some stretches later, you know, prepare for tomorrow."

"That's too bad," she said with a lift of her shoulders, "I was hoping you'd be up for a little fun? But if you're going to mope around here all day in your disgusting sweatpants, I'll go find someone else to have fun with."

"What'd you have in mind?"

"Ice cream, beer and two-stepping at Nashville North."

He brushed the corner of his mouth with his index finger and nodded. "In that order?"

Eden shrugged. "I'm easy, your choice."

"All right, beer and dancing first, ice cream later. How does that sound?"

"Good to me as long as you're not too sore to go dancing." Eden stood and took his hands in hers pulling him to a standing position in front of her.

"I'm never too sore to hold a beautiful woman in my arms." He twirled her in a circle and pulled her in close against his chest, his breath warm against her ear. "So when you said you were easy—"

"Don't even go there." She laughed and twisted to face the mischief dancing in his eyes and playing along the curve of his mouth.

RJ's subtle sense of humor was one of the reasons she'd fallen for him in the first place, along with his warm, sexy eyes and calm, tender nature. And she was falling all over again, her body responding to his touch like memory foam. A familiar tingle tugged gently at her heart urging her to give him another chance. Eden started at the thought. What was she thinking? No. No more chances for RJ. He was a part of her past and nothing more.

"Shame on you," she said as much to him as to herself, and swatted his hands from her waist. "Go put on some jeans, cowboy and take me dancing."

A half hour later, Eden rested her neck in her hands, her elbows perched atop the wooden table at Nashville North. Something wasn't right with RJ. The rodeo portion of Stampede had ended for the day and crowds of people were streaming inside the tent to score a table, party the night away with friends and dance to the live music. RJ was up at the bar paying for drinks and chatting with friends.

To anyone else she knew he appeared relaxed and comfortable. A slightly uneasy stance and rigid angle of his head signaled he was anything but. She remembered as an up and comer in the rodeo he'd perfected a humble, warm persona at a young age to hide the jumble of nerves jumping beneath his skin. It surprised her he wasn't more secure in his career considering his exposure and success on the circuit.

Funny how some things never changed.

Every time she was near him it was like traveling back through time and reliving every emotion. Touch. Glance. Back to a time when he really was the humble, warm man with whom she'd shared her body and everlasting love.

A low sigh shaped from misery and longing scuffed the back of her throat and whispered across her lips. Damn you, RJ. If Velvet hadn't ripped up her photo, she never would have learned she'd been his lucky charm all these years, never felt the surge of joy at being buried in his hugs or the felt the pain of what could never be again.

She'd worked too hard to leave the past where it belonged, and move forward in her career and possibly towards love with... well, with someone, maybe Jon. And if that didn't happen, love would come when it was right and not before. She knew she'd love RJ until the end of time, but she wasn't prepared to suffer until the end of time. Eden smiled. She had way too much self-esteem for that.

Velvet had confirmed she had the talent to succeed with her clothing design business and although the offer was now dead in the water, Eden was confident she wouldn't have accepted it anyway. Helping Kaitlin was her priority and she was more than content to manage the Western store over the next three years, expand her bank account, and concentrate on her designs and online presence. She was only twenty-three for heaven's sake; she had a lifetime to reach her dream.

"Cheers and a penny for your thoughts." RJ handed her a beer and they clanked cups.

"Hah, in Canada pennies are a thing of the past, at the very least you could offer me a nickel."

"A nickel it is. I don't mean to drink and run, but Velvet and Jesse just walked in and I don't want a confrontation. Do you mind if we leave?"

"You're going to run into them sooner or later. Why not make it sooner and get it over with?"

"Not today. Maybe tomorrow, after I win." He smiled and reached for her hand and squashed it against his stomach. "Besides, I have a deep hunger for ice cream."

"With a side of mini donuts?"

"And deep-fried pork belly?"

Eden wrinkled her nose. "That's gross."

"They're selling it on the grounds and you know what they say, don't knock it until you've tried it."

"You actually eat it?"

He grinned at her look of disbelief. "Nope, I said don't knock it until *you've* tried it."

"There you go, trying to be funny again." She slid off the stool and reached for his hand. "Let's go." She smiled, more for herself than RJ. She may not be in this relationship for the long haul anymore but it didn't mean they couldn't have fun for the rest of the day.

"Have you ever tasted anything so delicious?" Eden's eyelids fluttered as the last of the sugary confections melted in her mouth.

Somewhere in the distance shrieks of fear and delight echoed across the carnival midway, music blared and bells clanged, and carney's shouted 'WE HAVE A WINNER!' at the top of their lungs. RJ pushed the clatter from his mind and was lost in a fantasy of Eden's gorgeous lips. Plump red lips curved in a sugary dream and smudged with a dusting of powder. They were the lips of the most beautiful woman he had ever tasted. "Yeah," he whispered, "I have."

His lips parted in fond remembrance of flirty days and sultry nights and he leaned in for a stolen kiss.

"Are you avoiding me, RJ?"

Grabbed by a firm hand, he was snatched from Eden's lips and swung to face the intruder. Velvet. His eyes narrowed a fraction. It was always Velvet. "What are you talking about?"

"You walked out on me at Nashville North," she snarled, her eyes flashing angrily.

RJ sighed and placed a protective arm around Eden's shoulders. "We didn't walk out on you, Velvet, we were already leaving."

A malicious smile torched her lips. "Off to the ranch to see Auntie and Uncle and help them move?" She laughed cruelly as RJ's rigid form snapped to attention. "Remind them to take as much of their junk as they can carry because when the papers are signed and the ranch is mine and Daddy's, we plan to make a few changes."

"Such as?" he asked, feeling vaguely comforted by the presence of Eden's arm tightening around his waist.

"For starters we're going to level that disgusting farmstead and plant everything back to grass, and then we'll sell, at a profit of course. She arched a perfectly shaped eyebrow and smirked. "By the time we're done with your precious little property, no one will even remember the Benson ranch existed."

"Why are you doing this, Velvet? Your father doesn't want my uncle's ranch any more than you do."

"Why, sugar." She reached forward with her hand, the silk of her thumb massaging the prickly scruff beneath his chin. "If there's nothing here for you to come back to, you'll finally realize you belong in Texas with me. And," she said with a confident shrug, "if I can make a profit along the way, all the better."

RJ jerked away from her touch. "Why the hell do you want me?"

"You owe me." Her eyes blazed a sinister purple sheen. "I rescued you. I healed you. And despite what you may think, I financed you, too. Nobody dumps Velvet Blair and gets away with it. You're *my* lucky charm, RJ. And I'm not finished with you yet," she said, with a superior nod to Eden.

"Hmm." A lopsided grin lit his face. "Well, it looks like your luck just ran out. I closed the deal on the ranch this morning. It belongs to me now and just so you know, it's not for sale."

A passerby shoving a path through the crowded midway grounds accidentally jostled Velvet's elbow and she cursed at the bodily interruption. "I don't believe you." She sneered. "No one in their right mind would lend you a penny."

"You're right," he said, shooting Eden a wink and rubbing his chin thoughtfully, "especially in Canada."

"This is your fault," she spat. "He never would have left me if it wasn't for you—" She lunged at Eden, but RJ stepped in front of her bracing for the attack. He was taken completely off guard when Jesse Hancock moved forward and tugged Velvet away from them.

"Well, here you are," he drawled, resting his chin on Velvet's shoulder and wrapping her close against his chest. "I was wondering where you'd gotten to. Is this fella bother'n you, darlin'?"

"No." She sniffed haughtily, quickly recovering her composure and snuggling against him. "I only wanted to give RJ's friend a good-luck hug, and RJ wouldn't have it. He's half the man you are, Jesse, and she deserves to know what she's getting into."

"I'm sure she already knows." He laid a quick kiss against her neck. "Come on, forget about this cowboy. Your friends are waiting at Nashville North. Let's go have some fun." He nodded and tipped his hat." It'll be a pleasure whipping your ass tomorrow, RJ."

"Don't count on it, Jesse," RJ said as they retreated. "Oh, and Velvet... consider yourself paid in full."

Velvet angrily smoothed back her hair and flipped him the bird.

CHAPTER 24

"*Y*ou bought the ranch?" Eden's jaw dropped in surprise.

"Well, not exactly." He smiled at her stunned expression and chuckled. "I mean, who in their right mind would lend *me* money?" He slid his thumbs into his back pockets and slumped against the metal siding of the vendor selling mini donuts. "I probably should have told her I was *planning* to buy the ranch."

"But why didn't you?"

"To get her off my back and hopefully out of my life and besides, telling her I already owned it was extremely satisfying."

"What are you going to do if you can't get the money?"

He reached for her hands. "I'm not sure, but I am going to talk to Uncle Harold and tell him the truth about my situation. Maybe he'll hold off selling until I have enough money saved up and if that doesn't work, well, maybe I'll go work at Frazer's Western Wear in High River. I hear the assistant manager is hot."

She shook free of his hands. "Don't joke, this isn't funny."

"I know, but it doesn't look good for me, Edie, and I can't count on winning the hundred thousand tomorrow either. I hope I do. But pocketing the cash before you win is considered bad luck

148

and I've had my fill of that lately." He pushed his hat farther back on his head and massaged circles along his temples. "Man, it's noisy down here. Can we go somewhere quieter for ice cream?"

Eden tilted her head considering her options. Whether she liked it or not she was still attracted to RJ, still enjoyed spending time in his company. While he tried not to show it, worry and fatigue were evident in his every movement and she was concerned how it would affect his performance tomorrow. They'd both suffered more than enough drama at the hands of Velvet this week and RJ needed a friend he could count on. If spending time with him meant getting her heart broken all over again when he left, well, it was a risk she was willing to take. She could weep about it later.

"Come with me, RJ," she said, "I know just the place."

"You've got ice cream on the end of your nose," RJ said and quickly snatched his spoon away from her face, popping the remaining scoop of Caramel Butter Pecan into his mouth.

"Only because you put it there," she snorted, jostling his elbow and attacking him with her spoon, smearing a sticky streak across his cheek.

"Hey!" He brushed his cheek with his sleeve and dove towards her, pinning her against the end of her sofa and playfully lapping what was left of the ice cream from the tip of her nose. Eden wriggled, gasping for him to stop, her chest heaving with laughter as he licked a wet trail towards her ear.

"Stop it, that's gross!" She giggled, ducked her chin and shoved her hands up against his chest.

"Whoa!" He teetered and landed with a thud on the floor. "That's the smallest sofa."

"It's a loveseat, nerd. I don't have room for a sofa in here—" He grabbed her wrist and she tumbled on top of him. "No fair," she gasped, and ground her coppery head back and forth along the scruffy surface of his chin.

"No, it really isn't." And it wasn't because here she was again, plastered against him, syncing her breath and wrapping him in a cloud of wildflowers, her lovely hard nipples poking holes in his plan to take things slow and hopefully make her love him again, or at the very least like him.

"Hey? What's that noise?" A series of loud bangs from below rattled his nerves and the empty ice cream bowls wobbled precariously on the edge of the coffee table.

Eden giggled and lifted her head. "It's my downstairs neighbor. He hates noise. I guess we were being too loud." She rose, straddling his hips and rapped three times on the wooden floor. "It's our signal, promising I'll quiet things down."

"That's crazy. You need to move."

"What I need," she said, standing and extending her hand to pull him up, "is to win a million dollars. Then I can move."

"Not before we have a dance."

"And risk the wrath of 'Shrek'? My neighbor is an ogre," she said, pointing towards the floorboards, "he's going to get cranky."

"'Shrek' I can handle, it's you I'm worried about. I promised you a dance at Nashville North and never delivered," he said, with a grin on his lips and a sway of his hips. "Care to join me?"

Eden clasped her hands behind his neck and followed the teenage shuffle. "I was expecting a two-step. This is like high school without the music."

"I could sing for you."

"We don't need music that badly," she teased.

"Ouch, that hurts me, Edie, right here…" He removed his hand from the small of her back and placed it across his heart.

"There's a remedy for that, you know," she said. Cupping his face in her hands she slowly brought his mouth to hers and stole his breath away.

He groaned beneath her lips. Eden was kissing him, slowly and gently. She nipped at his bottom lip and he felt his heart ping, threatening to erupt in a messy flow of emotion. "Edie." He tore his lips from her kiss, his eyes flecked with desire and dotted with surprise. "I... uh, are you sure? I mean, you and Jon—"

"Shh." The silk of her fingertips gently silenced the questions brimming in his eyes and burning on his lips, "Shut up and kiss me, RJ."

SHE WAS KISSING him and drowning in a buttery pecan swirl. Eden tightened her grip, deliriously happy to be back in his warm embrace. His hands slid low, gently caressing the firm curve of her butt, his palms pressing firmly back towards her waist. Rough from years on the circuit, his hands dipped dangerously below the waist of her jeans, teasing her sensitive skin with callused pleasure. Eden gasped. He was barely touching her and she was already teetering close to the edge. She should stop. She should really stop. Stop him. Stop herself. Stop her brain from erasing the pain of the past and denial of their tenuous situation. If she was smart she'd shove him mercilessly out the door. RJ deepened his kiss and she moaned against his lips and pressed closer against the length of his body.

The heel of his boot clicked against the wall behind them, and they bumped awkwardly. "I think we're stuck," he said, his breath floating in heated waves against her cheek.

"Not stuck." She met his smoky gaze full on. "You're almost exactly where I want you." She reached for his hand and tugged him across the hall into the path of her queen-sized bed.

"Are you sure, Edie?"

She nodded, her arousal heightened ever further by the depth of his concern and she quickly resolved that if she could have one night with the only man she'd ever loved, she'd take it no matter what the consequences were tomorrow.

"Yeah," she said, playfully pushing him onto the end of the bed,

"I am." She nudged between his legs and moved wickedly between them. "You've got way too many clothes on, RJ." She swiftly unfastened the top button of his shirt and moved to the next, fingers flying towards the hem.

"Careful, Edie, this is one of my good shirts. If you don't slow down, you're going to rip it."

She smiled, finishing her quest to reveal his nakedness. "You seem to forget what I do for a living." She pushed his shirt over his broad shoulders and down his arms, unabashedly admiring his magnificent pecs. "Wow." She reached forward and brushed her palms against his chest, circling his razor sharp nipples and trailing a tentative finger along the hard rugged edges of his abs. "You must really work out—a lot."

RJ grinned and tugged at her waist. "Get over here."

"Not so fast, cowboy." She jerked beyond his reach. "Didn't your auntie tell you a gentleman always takes his boots off at the door. Shame on you, there's no place for horseshit on my beautiful white linens." She turned and wrestled off his right cowboy boot, fully conscious of his hands moving seductively over her ass and the low glow of heat flaring in her groin. RJ wrenched her back, his boot slipping from her grip and slamming against the wall.

He flipped her onto her back and lowered his head to her neck, nuzzling sweetly below her ear. "I forgot how bossy you are."

"MmmHmm." She rolled her bottom lip between her teeth and gazed hungrily in his eyes. "Take off your pants."

"Not before I take off yours." He flicked open the button on her jeans, and sank his hand below the zipper, slicing it wide as he reached between her legs. "Mmm. There are a lot of things I may have forgot about you, Edie, but this," he said, slipping a finger inside her slick folds, his voice hoarse against her ear, "isn't one of them. You're so wet... always so damn wet for me." Her body slid and bucked, muscles clenched tightly around him in a desperate need for more.

"Take off your pants," she grumbled feverishly, "I've been

waiting a lifetime to feel you inside me again and I'm exhausted waiting for you to get your shit together." His grin skimmed the soft, warm flesh against her cheek, and he claimed her mouth, deepening his kiss as her hips arched against him. In a slow patient withdrawal, his hands returned to her hips and tugged at the waist of her jeans. Her hips instantly rose towards him wriggling frantically to free herself from the clinging denim fabric.

"Oh, Edie." He groaned in deep appreciation at her near nakedness, his thumb a whispering trail along the silk of her thong. He slowly dipped his head, brushing his lips between her legs and tenderly flicking the tip of his tongue along the dampened sliver of cloth. A strangled sigh escaped her throat and RJ continued upwards, hands gently gripping the curves of her upper body as he tucked random kisses along the smooth line of her belly. "I've missed you so much, Edie."

"Jeans off. Now," she ordered breathlessly, unintentionally swatting the top of his head with crossed forearms in a desperate attempt to wiggle free of her t-shirt. "Argh, I'm stuck," she wailed, struggling helplessly beneath the thin cotton fabric snagged beneath her chin and sucked to her face.

"Stop it!" She floundered weakly but passionately, and nipped at his lips puckered grotesquely beneath the thin white tee. "Help me out of this!" she yelped and smacked him deliberately on the head. RJ leaned back, his elbow perched on the bed. "You're a vision of beauty, Edie, I gotta get a picture of this."

"Don't you dare!" Her arms flailed blindly towards him and he reached beyond her grasp, unfurled her from the tangled shirt and whipped it over her head.

"What?" she demanded heatedly, her hands moving swiftly through her hair anxiously trying to tame the static of her burnished halo.

"You," he stated simply, his serious brown eyes glued to the crackling intensity flying from her eyes and blotching her cheeks, "are the most beautiful woman I've ever met and I want you badly but I can't make love to you." Her lips parted in surprise and he slipped a coppery strand of hair behind her ear, flinching at the sudden disappointment flooding her features. "I didn't bring any condoms. I wasn't expecting us to—"

Eden's lips parted in relief. "Bedside table." Unclasping her bra, she tossed it to the floor followed by the silky slip of her thong and rolled up onto her haunches for an admiring view of RJ's gorgeous taut butt still wrapped in an unfortunate layer of faded denim. She released a deep breath and licked her lips. "Are you ever gonna get naked?"

He smiled at her from over his shoulder, flicked open the large silver buckle worn proudly on his belt from his winning performance at the Williams Lake rodeo and unzipped his pants. He swiftly removed his jeans and boxers and slowly turned to face her.

"Mmm, RJ, you're all growed up." She licked her top lip and reached out to leisurely stroke the length of his erection.

RJ groaned, and a rush of tingles shot straight through to her hands, her feather light strokes strangely abuzz, gently skimming along the length of his shaft and caressing his sensitive tip. He groaned again and she felt herself being tugged to her knees and crushed against his hot exposed chest. Their lips were mere inches away and she desperately wanted to kiss him. Lacing her fingers possessively around his neck, she pulled his head towards her and crushed his mouth against her lips, his woodsy, natural scent drifting and settling around her. Every inch of her skin roared with the blaze of a raging fire and she pulled him back against her, sinking their entwined bodies down into the soft down duvet.

"Make love to me, RJ," she moaned, sweetly tracing the crescent-shaped scar near his left eye with the tip of her tongue, surrendering her mind and soul to the happiness and joy that had been deprived from her for so many years. "I need to feel you inside me."

"Edie..." His breath rushed against her neck, his chest muscles pulsing against her small firm breasts and rock-hard nipples. "I've missed you, I—" A quick flick of her tongue parted his lips and she hungrily devoured his words. His hands roamed greedily along her curves, his fingers dipping into the warm welcoming wetness between her legs. "Edie." He buried his face against the glowing tangle of her hair spread like a wild flame across her pillow and slowly slid his fingers from the wetness, grabbing for the condom on the night stand.

He moved over her and lowered his mouth, nipping gently along the edge of her chin and stealing breathless kisses from her lips. Eden gasped, he was so beautiful and sexy and hard. She grasped his ass, squeezing the firm, solid lines of his cheeks and forcing his erection closer to her center. RJ lifted his head, held her gaze and swiftly slid deep inside.

This. Was. It. Eden gasped. He was wild and lusty and incredibly sexy. His bare skin moved seductively across her flesh, joining their love forever. It was everything she remembered and so much more, and she was completely gone, hips rocking, matching his depth and rhythm as his strokes intensified, faster, deeper and rocketing her over the edge.

CHAPTER 25

"*E*den Blue, I have a bone to pick with you."

"My name is Edie, not Ed, not Eden. Edie, E-d-i-e," she whispered sleepily, a happy smile curving her lips and tugging her back to dreamland. "At least that's what a certain cowboy I know calls me." She sighed contentedly, snuggling the small curve of her butt up against the warmth of his lower body. "Okay." She yawned. "I'll play, what's the bone?"

"Well, you insulted me last night," he said, his thumb and index finger firmly tweaking her closest nipple.

"Hey!" she cried, wiggling unsuccessfully to escape his arms and finally succumbing to his powerful embrace. "What'd I say?"

"You told me I was 'all growed up,'" he growled, his lips brushing over her ear.

"And?"

He tweaked her nipple again in response to the amusement spiking her voice, and was rewarded with a high-pitched squeak. "The fact is, I was all growed up when I left five years ago. I deserve an apology."

Eden teasingly swatted at his wandering fingers now tracing a tingling path along her belly towards the increasingly slick folds between her legs. "Mmm. Maybe so, RJ, but have you looked in the mirror lately?" She wriggled free and rolled towards him, palming his solid, muscled chest and callously tweaking the hard peaks of his nipples.

He jerked beneath the pinch of her fingers. "Ouch! Now I'm really insulted. You're treating me like a piece of meat. I believe it's called objectifying."

She tilted her head, eyes gleaming with laughter. "Ooo, big word for an itty-bitty bareback rider."

RJ chuckled and flopped onto his back dragging Eden along with him. "It's good to be home, Edie." He tenderly kissed the top of her head and gently smoothed her coppery strands, relieved the stress and tension tearing at his gut over the last couple of weeks was gone, completely evaporating the moment Eden had welcomed him back into her life. Her chest rose and fell in a gentle easy rhythm against his heart. He'd always believed Eden came from a humble place of honesty and he felt the essence of that goodness wash over him with each cleansing breath. If this wasn't love...

"RJ?" Eden lifted her head, raising her chin off his chest, her body supported by her elbows on each side of his body. "What are you going to do if you can't get the money to buy the ranch?"

"I'm not sure." His gaze locked with hers and he released a long low breath, troubled by the depth of emotion reflected back at him in her eyes. "I may have to go back to Texas and work on a ranch. I know a couple of guys who'll give me a job. I don't want to go, but it might be my only chance to get back on my feet."

"With Velvet?"

"Who?" he said, raising his eyebrows in mock question. Eden wrinkled her nose and RJ shrugged at his attempt to lighten the mood. "I'd be a long way from Velvet and Houston, Edie. You wouldn't have to worry." A lopsided grin tipped his mouth. "Hey, you could come with me. I mean, your work is portable, right? You can work anywhere."

Eden lowered her eyes and shook her head. "I can't, RJ." Tears and misery blurred the blue of her eyes. "I promised Kaitlin I'd manage the store."

"She could get someone else." He cupped the side of her face and stroked her cheek, "You have to come, I need you. This could be a new beginning for both of us."

"She's pregnant with twins, RJ, and she's sicker than a dog right now, that's why you haven't seen her. I can't leave her hanging, she's depending on me."

"Ok, well." He thrust a hand through his curls and gritted his teeth. "So, if I leave and you stay, how will I know you and Jon won't get back together?"

"Umm, well, you see, um." She cast him a guilt-ridden glance. "Remember at the mall when I told you I had a boyfriend?"

RJ narrowed his eyes. "Are you saying you lied? Jon's not your boyfriend?"

"Uh, Jon is more of a friend."

"Are you sure, because I saw the way you looked at each other and it seemed like there was way more between the two of you than you're saying. What's going on?"

"The truth is, I asked Jon to pose as my boyfriend so you wouldn't think I was a loser. I mean you blindsided me with the yellow thorn of Texas, I had to do something." Eden ginned. "So I borrowed gorgeous Jon to level the playing field and you know what, we really do like each other. He's a great guy and a wonderful friend and if things hadn't worked out the way they did with you and Velvet, there's a strong probability we'd be together right now."

"I'm glad you're not."

"What are we going to do, RJ? I don't want to lose you again."

Silent ropes of tension knotted along the base of his neck and travelled down his body, re-igniting the low flame of anxiety rising in his gut. "We'll figure it out, don't worry, Edie," he said, wiping the tears from her cheeks. He sucked in a deep breath trying to steady his breathing. "Shit, what time is it?" A grin creased his face. "I gotta kick Jesse Hancock's ass today."

"Oh!" Eden clasped her hands over her mouth and laughed. "I can't believe we almost forgot. You're gonna win today, RJ, I can feel it." She rolled her bottom lip between her teeth, her eyes glowing with pride. "With your talent and your good luck charm right in front of you, how could you lose?" And with the flush of reclaimed love lighting her face, she placed her lips on his chest and kissed a lasting memory into his heart.

CHAPTER 26

"*L*adies and Gentlemen... at this time, I'll ask you to please stand and remove your hats for the singing of the national anthem."

RJ stood proudly alongside his fellow competitors in the infield and pressed his cowboy hat against his chest. He gazed out over the arena trying to soak up every ounce of crackling energy and excitement sparkling from the sea of faces in the grandstand. The powerful strains of 'O Canada' floated somewhere in his subconscious below the layer of emotion pulsing through his veins and the heart-splitting pride of competing in front of Edie and his aunt and uncle.

Showdown Sunday. He still couldn't believe he was here. Being invited to the Calgary Stampede was a huge honor and presented him and every cowboy competing here today with a one hundred-thousand-dollar chance that could change their lives forever.

A pang of insecurity clutched at his gut. Battling against the best bareback riders in the world was incredibly overwhelming. RJ closed his eyes and gulped against the rage of nerves burning up his confidence.

Breathe. Uncle Harold was selling the ranch. *Release.* Velvet was threatening to destroy him and everyone in his life. *Repeat.* And he had no means to stop her.

An uncomfortable sensation rolled over his shoulder. He glanced fleetingly down the line of contestants right into Jesse Hancock's condescending smirk. It was like a knife against his throat.

Crap. Why was he letting Jesse get to him like this?

Edie was back in his life. *Breathe.* His fingers brushed the hand-painted feather attached to the band of his hat. *Release.* His good luck charm loved him. *Repeat.*

And the heat of her lips still thrilled against his heart. A wave of understanding washed over him and calmed the tension clawing at his gut. He wasn't riding to beat Jesse, he was riding for Edie and their future.

In a few minutes he'd be climbing over the chute onto the back of a big ole' buckskin with a familiar pattern he'd conquered twice this season. Steely Dan was tough, and predictable. A reel of their last encounter played like a movie through his mind. When Steely Dan left the chute he always veered to the left. His jumping pattern required big spur action, but he was a sweet ride and RJ had scored well into the high eighties on both performances. A smile curved his lips, he didn't want to count his winnings, but shit, Steely Dan was a sure thing.

"You're up, RJ," the chute boss yelled.

He placed a foot on either side of the chute and lowered himself onto the muscular back of a bucking horse he was destined to make history on. He worked his gloved hand under the rigid handle of the rigging, tugging and molding his fingers into position, and then scooted his hips tight against the handle. Steely Dan moved impatiently below him and he grabbed for the gate to steady himself. The faint scent of the freshly worked arena, the sweet aroma of manure and damp sweat wafting from the horse filtered up his nostrils, soothing his nerves and ramping his adrenaline. Spurs set high on the buckskin's shoulders, his arm cocked back and high, he inhaled deeply, nodded his head and braced himself for the ride of his life.

Somewhere in the distance someone shouted: "strong feet!" The gate swung open and Steely Dan burst from the chute, veering to the left as predicted, his hooves slamming hard against the dirt. RJ fell back, his spurs rolling down the buckskin's neck and snapping back up to the rigging—but RJ's feet kept flying. Steely Dan's left hoof slid sideways on the dirt—

RJ's head slammed against the solid ball of the horse's hindquarters and the bronc collapsed, skidding sideways on the infield floor trapping RJ beneath his girth.

It took a fraction of a second for him to realize Steely Dan wasn't getting up. A strangled shout for help ripped from his mouth and the thunder of boots descended quickly towards him and into the path of a brutally dangerous situation. RJ worked furiously to release his glove from the bind, barely conscious of the team of cowboys struggling to restrain the thrashing mound of muscle on top of him and keep Steely Dan from beating him to a pulp. The weight of the horse shifted and he was pulled out from under, shoved in the direction of the chutes, scattering for safety alongside the crew of cowboys who had helped in his rescue.

The crowd erupted in explosive applause as Steely Dan scrambled to his feet, angrily snorting and bucking his way around the infield. RJ steadied himself against the rail, flinching at the sight of his ride playing on the big screen. A buzz of adrenaline sailed through his limbs and his chest heaved with disappointment. His dream of winning Stampede vaporized as Steely Dan disappeared with a final kick down the runway.

"You okay, RJ?"

"Yeah." He nodded his assurance to the group of concerned cowboys gathered near his side. He sucked in an anxious breath, trying to stop the sinkhole swirling in his gut. His whole life hung in the hands of the judges. What the hell was taking them so long to decide the fate of his ride?

"That right there, ladies and gentlemen, is a testament to the danger of rodeo and the speed at which something can unexpectedly happen. But it also demonstrates the comradeship that exists within the rodeo community and the willingness to put their own lives in the face of danger to help a fellow competitor."

"Now the good news is," the announcer's solemn hue swung flawlessly into a positive beat, "is that both horse and rider are okay. Give them another round of applause."

The crowd roared its approval and a huge grin broke across RJ's face. He lifted his hat and smiled.

"It looks like we haven't seen the last of RJ Stoke today, folks. Congratulations cowboy," he said, his voice booming across the stadium, "*you've got yourself a re-ride!*"

"It's been an exciting afternoon for the bareback event so far ladies and gentlemen, and it's not over yet! Here's how things look going into the final ride. Kyle White is sitting in third place at eighty–six and a half points, followed by Casey Mason with an eighty-eight, and no one has to tell you about the cowboy coming off one of the most spectacular rides we've witnessed so far... you know his name... your leader, Jesse Hancock, sitting in first place with a huge lead of *ninety points!*" The announcer's voice sank to a low growl. "But can he hold it? Well, there's only one way to find out," he said with a chuckle. "RJ Stoke is back in chute one. Let's see if he has better luck on his re-ride than he did with the first one."

RJ drew a long deep breath and lowered himself onto the back of a horse he knew little about. Midnight Kiss was a relative newcomer this season, hailing from the Calgary Stampede Ranch and building a reputation as the rankest bronc in rodeo history. She was a strong black mare, wild and unpredictable, and with a flare for elimination, having thrown more of her competitors than had ridden her. With Jesse Hancock sitting in first place at ninety points and Midnight Kiss already trying to ram him apart in the chute…he was so screwed.

RJ quickly touched the fingers of his glove against his lips, tapped the feather on his hat and slid his hand over his heart. "I'm gonna need your help more than ever on this one, Edie," he murmured, "at least help me win some decent day money."

He shoved his glove into the rigging, tugging and shaping his fingers around the rigid handle, striving for the perfect curl. Satisfied the bind would hold, he snugged up tight against the rigging and braced his knees against the rippling shoulders of the majestic beast pawing at the dirt beneath him. RJ drew in one last deep breath, cocked his arm back and nodded his head.

"Hold on to your hats folks, for a wild, wild ride! Remember, the higher the horse jumps, the harder he kicks, the more points RJ's going to score! Hang on tight, cowboy, because Midnight Kiss is on a mission and she's a wishin' for you to kiss the ground!"

Midnight Kiss exploded from the gate, and RJ held tight, knees gripped against her neck, heels dug deep above the shoulders. At the first thud of the mare's hooves striking the dirt he fell back, his spurs beating down her neck and snapping back to the shoulders, his free arm stretched way back, fighting and absorbing the ripping impact of each powerful jerk. Midnight Kiss spun violently to the right and RJ held tight, spurs whipping back to the rigging, toes out opening himself to the elements, his body slamming along the bronc's broad back, chaps flying, blood pounding, his spirits soaring. RJ Stoke was in the house and in complete control of the most ornery horse the Stampede had to offer. He was loose, fluid and having the ride of his life.

The timer buzzed. Eight seconds. It seemed like a lifetime. The crowd exploded with excitement. RJ freed his hand from the rigging and swung an arm around the pick-up man. He dropped to his feet and dashed for the safety of the chutes, away from the rage of Midnight Kiss's stubborn exit back to the runway. He accepted the slaps on his back and hollered congratulations with the biggest smile his face could hold. Even if Jesse beat him, the adrenaline shooting through his body was enough for him to know it wasn't the security of a big fat check he'd lost. No, he'd conquered Midnight Kiss and regained his confidence. No matter the outcome, with or without the ranch, he was pumped for a future with Eden at his side.

"Folks, it looks like we have a fight to the finish! RJ, you threw down the gauntlet and accepted the challenge with class, young man, and I must say with one of the prettiest rides this afternoon, but is it enough? Ninety points is gonna be hard to beat, cowboy." The announcer paused then said, "Here we go, looks like the judges have made a decision."

"The cowboy walking away from Showdown Sunday's Bareback competition at this year's Calgary Stampede, with ninety and a half points is your winner. Let's hear it for RJ STOKE!"

The arena erupted in wild applause. RJ pumped his arms in the air and stepped forward. "Not so fast." Jesse Hancock grabbed his arm and blocked his path. "Hell of ride today, RJ, but I just wanted to let you know, I still think you're a fluke." He grinned, slapped RJ on the back and moved aside.

RJ stepped forward, bathed in the crowd's wild adulation. He smiled widely, tipped his hat to the audience and flung it high above the arena floor. Hell ya! He pumped his fist into the air. He'd won Stampede! His aunt and uncle waved wildly from the bleachers reserved for family and friends with Eden beside them, jumping and hollering with happiness and shining like a brilliant star.

Eden was the real prize of the day, not the hundred thousand. RJ lifted his fingers to his lips, placed them against his heart and pointed towards the stands.

CHAPTER 27

"*A*re you sure RJ didn't send you a text? Can you please check again?"

"Oh, hon." Auntie Rae cradled Eden's head against her chest, smoothing her hair and gently wiping at the tears wetting her cheeks. "We haven't heard anything since last night. When did he leave?"

"I don't know for sure." Her eyes glistened with moisture, threatening to spill at any moment. "We went back to my place after supper last night. RJ was so happy, we were both so happy, and, I mean, we had the most special…" She closed her eyes and rolled her bottom lip between her teeth. "I'm sorry," she whispered, a sob catching in her throat. "He was gone when I woke up, his clothes, his bag, everything was gone."

Between gentle hugs and heart-wrenching sobs, Auntie Rae haltingly guided her from the front hall and onto a kitchen chair where Eden collapsed and sobbed quietly into her hands.

"Have a sip, dear." Auntie Rae settled on the chair beside her and pressed a glass of water in her hands. "Did he leave you a note? A text? Anything?"

"Only a text." Her voice wavered, her eyes filled with tears. "He said he loved me but his life was a mess and he needed to figure things out. I texted him back but he won't answer my texts and I'm so worried. I thought he might be here, but he's not and you don't know where he is and I'm worried he's gone back to Texas with Velvet. Ohhh." She gasped sharply, panting with ragged breaths. "Do you think he ran off with Velvet?"

"No." Auntie Rae slapped the hard, wooden surface. "No, not with Velvet. He'll be back, I promise."

"Got coffee on, Rae?" Uncle Harold strode through the door to the kitchen and immediately headed to the sink to wash up. "I thought that was your car out front, Eden, did you bring RJ with ya," he said, then paused and chuckled, "or is he still out cold sleeping off a hangover?"

"Harold!"

"What?" He hung the towel on a hook beside the sink, and pulled the coffee maker across the countertop. "I assume he celebrated long after we left last night. Can't blame him, that was a hell of a ride yesterday, I'm still bursting with pride. There," he said, and returned the coffee tin to the cupboard, "coffee should be ready in a few minutes. Now, what are you two ladies up to?" He glanced at them. "Oh, damn."

"RJ's gone, Harold. Eden came out to see if he was here."

"Gone?" He shook his head. "Are you sure? Hmm, that doesn't sound right to me, where would he go?"

"He's been gone all morning, won't answer his texts or phone. Eden's worried he left with Velvet and is on his way back to Texas."

"Oh boy, I sure hope not." He folded his arms and slumped forward, the sleeves of his denim shirt scuffing the worn wooden surface. "That woman's a heap a trouble if there ever was one. Son of a bitch." He released a long slow breath. "I never should have interfered and sent RJ off to school." He gritted his teeth and scowled. "The confrontation he had with your father didn't help either. I'm sorry, Eden, this is all my fault."

"Our fault, Harold, I'm as much to blame as you," Auntie Rae said, reaching across the table with a reassuring touch of her hands.

Silence descended across the table. Eden swallowed hard, eyes scarred with questions. "What are you talking about?"

"RJ didn't tell you?"

"Harold, go pour the coffee." Auntie Rae slid her fingers down the side of Eden's hair and tucked a silky strand behind her ear. "You are so dear to our hearts, Eden, I hope you can forgive us but at the time we thought we were doing the right thing." A wisp of a smile tugged at the corners of her mouth. "Young love is a beautiful thing. I can't tell you how much Harold and I enjoyed watching you and RJ together. It was such fun having teenagers around, laughing and helping us out on the ranch. You, Kaitlin and RJ put a lot of joy—"

"—and a whole pail full of worry."

"—into our lives. Thanks, Harold." She plucked two steaming mugs of coffee off the tray he'd placed on the edge of the table and handed one to Eden, pouring a generous amount of cream into both. "Yes, worry too. RJ wasn't the only one learning a new way of life." She lifted the thick white ceramic mug to her lips. "Mmm, well now, that hits the spot."

Eden sipped from the cup, craving relief, but the strong hot liquid only burned her throat and coiled acridly in her stomach. "What happened?"

"It wasn't hard to see how serious the two of you were getting, Eden, and we were concerned about your futures. RJ didn't have any plans other than working on the ranch and going to rodeos. Yes, he'd be busy, but he'd still have time on his hands and I'm not sure he understood how busy *you* were going to be. Trying to fit school around a part- time job and a full-time boyfriend was a recipe for disaster in our eyes."

"We were down in New Mexico," Uncle Harold continued, "at the high school rodeo finals when we came up with the idea of sending RJ to college."

"Your idea?"

"I'm surprised he didn't tell you. We were approached by several scouts who were looking for up-and-coming bareback riders to add to their university teams. Rae and I hit it off immediately with the fella from Sam Houston. We started on the paperwork when we got home."

"RJ never mentioned it."

"RJ didn't know." Uncle Harold said. "Wish I could change that."

"All we could see," Auntie Rae interjected, "were two young people we cared so much about headed for heartache. This was our solution. We hoped you'd figure out a way to continue your relationship long distance. It's so much easier these days to keep in touch."

Eden's heart sank, the sharp claws of dread tearing up her throat. "What did my father have to do with this?"

"Digger was a little drunk." Uncle Harold grimaced at the lack of empathy lining Eden's face. "He accused RJ of forcing you to have sex with him."

"But that's not true."

"We know." Auntie Rae scraped the legs of her chair closer to Eden and wrapped a comforting hug around her shoulders. "Your father made some threatening comments towards RJ. I don't know if he would have carried through with any of them, but we were worried about his safety."

"And that's why RJ left? Why wouldn't he tell me?" Tears brimmed from her eyes and slid down her cheeks. "We could have worked things out."

"RJ was concerned more for your safety than his own and I'm afraid we convinced him it would be in your best interest and his, too, if he left for college in Texas. I'm sorry, Eden, but you were both so young and we never once thought he'd break up with you."

"I wish he would have told me." She sighed and rested her head on Auntie Rae's shoulder. "Sorry about my dad. I always wondered why he claimed he was the one who broke us up. It all makes sense now." Eden slid from Auntie Rae's embrace and leaned her arms on the table, her eyes haunted with misery. "But what I still don't understand is what happened between last night and this morning to make RJ leave *this time?*"

"WELL, Polly, it looks like it's just you and me again. Thought I'd stop and say goodbye before I left for home." Eden scrubbed the hair around Polly's neck with the tips of her fingers. There wasn't anything she didn't love about the smell of a horse. Sweet hay and sunshine musk, cracked leather, and the overpowering perfume of a certain cowboy... Eden sighed, well maybe there was one smell she wasn't crazy about anymore. "Never fall in love with a cowboy, Polly, they just love you and leave. But I guess you already know that, huh? RJ left you, too."

Polly whinnied and shook her head, her mane slapping the top of Eden's head. "I know, shame on me. I tried to play the friend card, but he reeled me in, inch-by-inch with his bad boy smile and those crazy, beautiful eyes, and geez, Polly, did you see his body?" Polly snickered and tapped her on the shoulder with her muzzle. That was why women loved horses, she thought, they smelled good and were your friend no matter what, especially when you carried a treat. Eden closed her eyes and smiled sadly into the warmth of the horse's neck.

The crunch of gravel along the driveway crackled under the weight of an approaching vehicle and caught her attention. Eden closed Penny's stall door and cautiously made her way to a window overlooking the yard. RJ had pulled his one-ton diesel to a stop in front of the house. She saw his head jerk in a double take at the sight of her vehicle, but any emotion playing on his face was hidden by the brim of his cowboy hat.

Eden absently drummed her fingers across the sack of feed, stacked near the barn door. Was RJ happy she was here? She wrinkled her nose. Or disappointed? He'd bounded up the steps to the house like a ten-year-old, surely that meant he was happy.

"RJ's come home, Polly," she called towards the back of the barn. "What do you think I should do?" The horse snickered and pawed her response in the dirt. "That's what I think, too, girl." A wide grin spread across Eden's face, "that's what I think, too."

∼

"RJ Stoke, where do get off disappearing like that!" Auntie Rae met him at the kitchen door, anger fuming from every pore.

He screeched to a halt, eyes startled and wide. "Uh, like what?"

"You know darn well what I mean. Where have you been? Eden's been calling and texting you all morning and half the afternoon. We all thought you'd hooked up with Velvet again and left the country!"

"Wait a minute, Eden never called." He pulled out his phone, text after text from Eden scrolled up the screen. Five missed calls. Shit. He'd turned his phone off before his meeting at the Farm Credit office this morning and forgot to turn it back on. He lifted an eyebrow and shrugged sheepishly at his aunt and uncle. "I got the loan—"

"—if you don't learn to communicate better you're going to lose that girl for good!" Auntie Rae jammed her fists onto her hips, angry puffs of air blasting from her lungs. "Now, where did you say you were?"

"He got the loan," Uncle Harold said quietly and tapped her lightly on the arm.

"To buy the ranch?" RJ nodded and she flew into his arms. "Oh son, I'm so happy." She drew back, her face wreathed in smiles, eyes shining with tears. "We honestly thought you'd left."

"Sit down and give us the details," Uncle Harold said, rescuing RJ from his wife's stranglehold and ushering him to the table. "What did they say? I would have gone with you if you'd asked."

"Thanks, Uncle Harold, I know, but I felt this was something I needed to do myself. I haven't been completely honest with the two of you since coming home." He leaned forward and clasped his hands. "The reason I was trying to stall you into selling the ranch is because I don't have any money. I know—" He silenced his aunt with a wave of his hand.

"I've been winning consistently on the circuit all year, but I've been living much higher than the balance in my bank account. I have some money saved, enough to get out of my lease on my apartment in Houston and make a few truck payments, but other than that, I'm basically broke. If I hadn't won yesterday, I'd have to go back to Texas and find some work."

"With Velvet?"

"No, not with Velvet. Don't look so worried, Auntie Rae. Velvet and I are finished. I've got my eye on a gorgeous redhead now."

"So, what did Farm Credit say?" Uncle Harold interrupted.

"We talked about the price of the ranch and the sizable balance sitting in my bank account thanks to my win, and they guaranteed I qualify for a loan. I made an appointment for next week to talk things through and see what paperwork they need and things like that. I'd appreciate it if you'd come with me, Uncle Harold, your advice means the world to me."

"I believe this calls for a celebration!" Uncle Harold said with a smile spread from ear to ear.

"That's what I thought, so I picked up a case of beer in town. It's in my truck, I'll go get it—"

"Not so fast." Auntie Rae pinned RJ's hand to the table along with a cold hard stare. "Young man you have some explaining to do. I can understand spending the morning trying to get a loan and stopping somewhere for a bite to eat, but what I can't understand is how you could possibly think it was okay to leave Eden's without a word this morning, go about your business and then come out here without phoning her first. You better have a good story, son, because if Eden doesn't lay a licking on you, I will. Where else have you been?"

"Well, I was hoping to share this with Edie first but—" He reached into his pocket and pulled out a small box. "Open it."

"Oh, my word." Auntie Rae's lips parted at the stunning gold and silver engagement ring sparkling back at her. "RJ," she sighed. "It's beautiful. I could kiss you!"

"Before or after you lay a beating on me?" he replied with grin.

"Are you sure it's not too soon, son, I mean you've only been back a couple of weeks."

"Better than being five years too late, Uncle Harold." He scanned the kitchen, through the doorway and into the hall. "Where is Edie anyway?"

"She's—what the heck's that noise?" A loud series of horn blasts were followed by revving and the deep rumble of a diesel truck. Auntie Rae jumped up from the table and hurried to the kitchen window. "Someone's got your truck, RJ."

He grabbed his hat off the table, ran towards the door and flew onto the veranda. "What the—?"

"Hey, RJ." Eden popped her head out the driver side window of his truck and leaned her arms across the top of the door. "They're playing our song on the radio."

RJ narrowed his eyes, set his cowboy hat low over his forehead, and slowly lowered his boots down to the first step.

"That's a pretty shiny buckle you're wearing, cowboy."

"Thank you, ma'am." He skipped down the last couple of steps and leisurely wandered towards her. "I just won it at the Calgary Stampede."

"Not bad for an itty-bitty bareback rider."

He smiled and leaned towards her. "I didn't realize we had a song. What's it about?"

"Well, if you listen closely you'd know it's about going on a date in a truck down by the creek."

"We've never gone to the creek in a truck before."

"But we've gone to the creek," she said cheekily, "and I wore a white summer dress and we drank beer."

"I hate to tell you this, but you're not wearing a white dress."

Eden glanced at her t-shirt and jeans. "Hmm. You're right," she said, "but I've got the beer." She pointed to the case RJ had brought with him from town.

RJ arched a brow and grinned. "Does this mean we're gonna get naked?"

Eden smiled broadly and clicked open the door of the truck. "Get in, cowboy."

"Just a sec." He turned towards his aunt and uncle who were leaning on the veranda, eavesdropping on their exchange. "Would you mind if Edie and I went down to the creek for a while?" he said, and patted the small square box buried inside his front jean pocket.

"You two go ahead, we'll be just fine, won't we, Harold?"

"Scoot over, Edie." He climbed in beside her and kissed her plump, red lips. "We've got a lot to talk about."

AUNTIE RAE and Uncle Harold leaned contentedly on the railing of the deck and watched the glow of tail lights on RJ's truck disappear below the hill in the pasture.

Uncle Harold squeezed Auntie Rae intimately around her waist and pecked her on the lips. "Well, like I said before, this calls for a celebration."

"It most certainly does," she said, and playfully wriggled out of his arms. She strolled over to the porch swing and sat down, "How about a nice cold beer?"

Uncle Harold flicked the latch on the screen door and comically wiggled his eyebrows. "Does this mean we're gonna get naked?"

A gentle breeze skipped across the veranda, wrapping her in the heavenly scent of wildflowers. "It most certainly does." She flashed a wink at Harold through the open kitchen window and smiled. Love was definitely in the air.

WOMEN OF STAMPEDE SERIES

Saddle up for the ride! The Women of Stampede will lasso your hearts! If you love romance novels with a western flair, look no further than the Women of Stampede Series. Authors from Calgary, Red Deer, Edmonton and other parts of the province have teamed up to create seven contemporary romance novels loosely themed around The Greatest Outdoor Show on Earth... the Calgary Stampede. Among our heroes and heroines, you'll fall in love with innkeepers, country singers, rodeo stars, barrel racers, chuckwagon drivers, trick riders, Russian Cossack riders, western-wear designers and bareback riders. And we can't forget our oil executives, corporate planners, mechanics, nursing students and executive chefs. We have broken hearts, broken bodies, and broken spirits to mend, along with downed fences and shattered relationships. Big city lights. Small town nights. And a fabulous blend of city dwellers and country folk for your reading pleasure. Best of all, hearts are swelling with love, looking for Mr. or Miss Right and a happily ever after ending. Seven fabulous books from seven fabulous authors featuring a loosely connected theme—The Calgary Stampede.

AUTHOR REQUEST

Your opinion matters.

Review this book on your favorite book site, review site, blog, or your own social media properties, and share your opinion with other readers.

Your review means a lot to me and I thank you for sharing your insights into my debut novel.

C.G. Furst.

ABOUT C.G. FURST

Raised in a small town in Saskatchewan, C.G. Furst never imagined she would marry a handsome farmer from Alberta and end up trying to corral escaped pigs in her high heels. Spurred by her love of the written word and the power of imagination she studied journalism in Calgary and became a copywriter for radio. Happily retired from chasing pigs, she now spends her days dreaming up new and impossible ways for the characters in her books to fall in love. C.G. Furst farms with her husband, two sons and families near the beautiful Drumheller Badlands.

 facebook.com/C.G.Furst